‖‖‖‖‖‖‖‖‖‖‖‖‖‖‖‖‖‖‖‖‖‖

◁ **P9-CBS-801**

DEATH OF A CUPCAKE QUEEN

Suddenly rising above the din of the dogs barking was a man's anguished cry.

It was coming from the kitchen.

The swinging doors burst open and Charles McNally, his arms raised in the air, his face a frozen mask of grief and horror, stumbled out.

He could barely speak.

He just pointed toward the kitchen.

Leading the charge, Hayley dashed across the room with Liddy, Nykki and Sabrina close on her heels. They were followed by a swarm of other startled and curious classmates. They all poured into the kitchen and stopped short at the grisly sight.

Ivy Foster was lying face down on the floor surrounded by her signature butter cream cupcakes as her devoted pack of tiny toy poodles named after the seven dwarves danced around her body yipping and yapping and howling in a panicked frenzy . . .

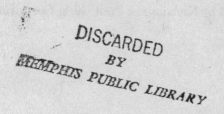

DISCARDED
BY
MEMPHIS PUBLIC LIBRARY

Books by Lee Hollis

DEATH OF A KITCHEN DIVA

DEATH OF A COUNTRY FRIED REDNECK

DEATH OF A COUPON CLIPPER

DEATH OF A CHOCOHOLIC

DEATH OF A CHRISTMAS CATERER

DEATH OF A CUPCAKE QUEEN

Published by Kensington Publishing Corporation

A Hayley Powell
Food & Cocktails Mystery

DEATH OF A CUPCAKE QUEEN

LEE HOLLIS

KENSINGTON PUBLISHING CORP.

http://www.kensingtonbooks.com

KENSINGTON BOOKS are published by

Kensington Publishing Corp.
119 West 40th Street
New York, NY 10018

Copyright © 2015 by Rick Copp and Holly Simason

All rights reserved. No part of this book may be reproduced in any form or by any means without the prior written consent of the Publisher, excepting brief quotes used in reviews.

If you purchased this book without a cover, you should be aware that this book is stolen property. It was reported as "unsold and destroyed" to the Publisher and neither the Author nor the Publisher has received any payment for this "stripped book."

All Kensington Titles, Imprints, and Distributed Lines are available at special quantity discounts for bulk purchases for sales promotions, premiums, fund-raising, and educational or institutional use. Special book excerpts or customized printings can also be created to fit specific needs. For details, write or phone the office of the Kensington special sales manager: Kensington Publishing Corp., 119 West 40th Street, New York, NY 10018, attn: Special Sales Department, Phone: 1-800-221-2647.

Kensington and the K logo Reg. U.S. Pat & TM Off.

ISBN-13: 978-0-7582-9453-1
ISBN-10: 0-7582-9453-0
First Kensington Mass Market Edition: June 2015

eISBN-13: 978-0-7582-9454-8
eISBN-10: 0-7582-9454-9
First Kensington Electronic Edition: June 2015

10 9 8 7 6 5 4 3 2 1

Printed in the United States of America

Chapter 1

Sabrina Merryweather was not the kind of woman you kept waiting for long. And Hayley was panic-stricken that she was already a half-hour late meeting her for an after work cocktail. Which explained how the back left tire of Hayley's Kia had just run up over the curb as she tried to quickly parallel park outside her brother Randy's bar, Drinks Like a Fish.

Hayley had been delayed at the office by an irate caller complaining about his name being misspelled in today's *Island Times* Police Beat column.

Seriously?

You want accuracy in the report of your Driving Under the Influence conviction?

Unbelievable.

Hayley checked her watch as she jumped out of the car and slammed the door shut. She dashed forward but was slung back suddenly by something snagging against her shoulder blade. She had been in such a hurry she didn't notice she had shut her bag inside the car.

The leather strap attached to the bag nearly dislocated her shoulder.

Hayley lost her balance and landed butt first on the pavement, her arm still dangling from the now limp strap.

She composed herself and casually glanced around to make sure no one had seen her embarrassing pratfall.

No such luck.

A couple of gum-chewing skateboarders in shorts hanging low enough to see the label of their Jockey underwear, nudged each other with their elbows and guffawed at Hayley, who was now using the strap to haul herself up on her feet.

She hit the unlock button on her remote, slowly opened the car door, and daintily removed her faux Fendi bag that had been trapped inside.

As the snickers and giggles a few feet away persisted, Hayley brushed herself off, locked her car again, and marched inside the bar, head held high.

God, it was only Monday.

She found Sabrina sitting alone at a table next to the wall, sipping a cocktail, a bright smile on her face.

Whatever happy pill she was on, Hayley wanted a prescription.

Pronto.

Sabrina had left her post as county coroner months ago after her husband filed for divorce in order to reassess her life and figure out where she wanted to go from here. Since that time, Hayley hadn't seen much of her at all, which to be truthful, wasn't such a bad thing considering Hayley had never been all that fond of her former high school nemesis Sabrina in the first place. Although Sabrina's memory of her astonishingly bad behavior back then was fuzzy at best, Hayley had a far more clear-eyed picture of Sabrina's past cruelties. But after seeing a self-help segment on the *Today Show* about how letting go of grudges helped you live longer, Hayley tried her best to forgive and forget.

Or at least forgive.

Forget?

Never.

When Sabrina called Hayley earlier in the day to suggest they meet for a drink and catch up after she got off work, Hayley just didn't have the energy to come up with an excuse not to go.

So she just said, *yes.*

One drink.

After all, she'd be lying if she said she wasn't at least a little bit curious to know what Sabrina had been up to all these months.

She had heard rumors.

One person told her that Sabrina took a trip

to see the Seven Wonders of the World but got waylaid in Machu Picchu with a stomach virus before giving up and coming home only having seen one wonder.

Another said she was launching her own medical practice again in Bangor, which was one hour north of the island.

There was also the Debbie Downer who insisted Sabrina had never fully recovered from her divorce and was holed up in her house crying over her leftover frozen wedding cake like some demented, haggard, jilted bride from an old Charles Dickens novel.

Hayley knew that last one was an outright lie because the Sabrina who was beaming from ear to ear as she sat down across from her at a corner table was a far cry from the emotional car wreck some of her detractors were making her out to be.

"Hayley, you *must* have a sip of this Peanut Butter Cup Martini. It is so decadently delicious, you will just die!" Sabrina cooed as she pushed the glass by its stem over in front of Hayley.

"Let's hope not," Hayley said, lifting the glass and taking a tiny sip.

There was no arguing her point.

The drink was orgasmic.

"Kudos to your brother for another to-die-for cocktail recipe," Sabrina said, retrieving the glass back from Hayley and downing another gulp as she closed her eyes and savored the taste.

Hayley noticed a half-empty bottle of Sam Adams on the table. "Is someone else joining us?"

Sabrina popped her eyes back open and nodded, excited. "Yes. A friend. He's in the men's room."

"I see. And he's just a *friend*?"

A spurt of giggles escaped Sabrina's lips. She turned her face slightly away like an embarrassed school girl. Hayley couldn't remember Sabrina being so coquettish and demure.

She had suddenly gone from Dickens to a full-fledged Bronte heroine.

"Well, now you've certainly gotten my attention," Hayley said, smiling as she signaled to her brother behind the bar to bring over her usual Jack and Coke.

Randy gave her a wave and then grabbed a bottle of whiskey off the shelf.

"Is he local? Is it someone I know?" Hayley asked Sabrina, who was now dragging her fingertip across the rim of her martini glass gathering up the chocolate that lined it and then sliding her finger into her mouth and licking it off.

"No. I met him when I was visiting my sister in San Diego a few months ago. We were having lunch at an outdoor cafe in the Gas Lamp district and he jogged by. Our eyes met. But he kept going. It was a fleeting fantasy on my part. How could this strapping hunk of pure masculinity ever be interested in *me*? But then, without warning, he doubled back and introduced himself. My sister asked him to join us and he did! We've been inseparable ever since!"

Hayley glanced up to see a young man, not far past the legal drinking age, walking from the restrooms back toward their table.

This couldn't be him.

He was striking.

Black hair.

Gorgeous smile.

And he was covered in tattoos.

His arms.

The back of his hands.

And what Hayley could see of his smooth bronzed chest through his open silk white shirt that he wore with the sleeves rolled up to his elbows.

He wore thick black glasses and had two perfectly round holes in his ear lobe.

He was a sight to behold.

Hayley normally wasn't a big fan of body art and piercings. But this kid, this lean yet muscled Adonis, wore it so well.

When he smiled, it was as if the whole bar was suddenly bathed in a heavenly light.

Hayley's heart fluttered.

Not because she was attracted to him.

This was male beauty in its finest form and she was just appreciating it.

Oh, who was she kidding?

Of course she was attracted to him.

But he was almost young enough to be her son.

He stopped at the table and massaged Sabrina's shoulders. She melted at his touch. Her face turned crimson and out came another girlish giggle.

"You must be Hayley. I've been anxious to meet you. Mason Cassidy," the Adonis said in a deep baritone voice.

Hayley stood up and held out her hand, but Mason brushed it away and enveloped her in a tight hug. She could feel his rock hard chest as he squeezed her body tightly into his.

After releasing her from his iron grip, Mason gave her a playful wink. "Sorry. I'm a big hugger."

Oh, this kid was good.

Hayley suddenly found herself giggling.

It was contagious.

They both took a seat at the table.

His bright smile still blinded both of them.

Randy nearly walked into an adjacent table as he delivered Hayley's cocktail, his eyes glued to the handsome stranger. Somehow he managed to set it down in front of her without spilling too much of it.

"Thank you, Randy," Hayley said.

Randy never once looked at her. He was staring at the painted god with a laserlike focus. "Can I get you another beer?"

Mason picked up the bottle and examined it. "I'm not even halfway through this one yet. Are you trying to get me drunk?"

He winked at Randy, whose knees nearly buckled.

"Why? What would happen if I got you drunk?"

"Thank you, Randy. I think we're fine for now," Hayley said, placing a hand on his hip and giving him a subtle yet forceful send off.

"Just yell if you need anything, and I do mean *anything*!" he called out as he walked back behind the bar.

"For heaven's sake, Randy, you have a husband!" Hayley called after him.

"I may be happily married, but that doesn't mean I'm dead! There's no harm in window shopping even if I'm not going to buy anything!"

"So you two met in San Diego?" Hayley asked.

"Yes, she swept me off my feet," Mason said, cupping the back of Sabrina's neck and pulling her close so he could plant a soft, sweet kiss on her cheek.

"Mason works as a high diver at Sea World. He swims with porpoises. How sexy is that?" Sabrina said, squealing so high Hayley was surprised their glasses didn't shatter.

"Wow, that's very impressive," Hayley said.

Truly impressed.

"Yes, he trained as an acrobat and even worked in a couple of those Cirque Du Soleil shows in Las Vegas. So you can just imagine how limber he is when it comes to you know what!" Sabrina said, now lowering her voice to the point where it was almost Kathleen Turner husky in order to make her point.

"Yes, I can. So there's no need to explain . . ."

"Neither of my fuddy-duddy former husbands had the tactile grace that Mason brings to the bedroom. Hell, Jerry sprained his back just coming from the toilet to the dresser where he keeps his condoms. We hadn't even started yet!"

Mason nuzzled Sabrina's neck with the tip of his nose. "You are so cute."

"You know, Hayley, I never would have met Mason if I hadn't quit my job as county coroner. That was the best decision I have ever made."

"I'm so happy for you, Sabrina. Really, I am."

Hayley had to remind herself she, too, was blissfully happy dating the handsome town vet, Dr. Aaron Palmer.

Aaron was certainly a keeper.

Her relationship with him was an unexpected gift that she treasured.

But like her brother said, she wasn't dead.

Mason Cassidy, with his caramel complexion, suave manner, and lovely features, was certainly fun to look at and admire.

Good for Sabrina.

She deserved a little happiness after two ugly divorces.

Sabrina clasped Mason's hand and turned to Hayley. "You know, I seriously considered skipping out on our high school reunion this year even though I've been on the planning committee. I just couldn't bear the thought of my former classmates judging me and whispering behind my back about my two failed marriages and collapsed career. But now, with Mason by my side, I think I'm ready to face anyone. Even those mean bitches who were so rotten to us during high school. Am I right, Hayley?"

Hayley was speechless.

Rotten to *us*?

Sabrina was the kind of ultimate mean girl who literally inspired the best-selling guide to adolescent torture, *Queen Bees and Wannabes*!

Hayley nodded, deciding it was best not to poke a hole in Sabrina's happy mood.

"I am ready to introduce the new Sabrina Merryweather to the world in all her glory! I can just feel it! This reunion is going to be history-making!"

Sabrina had no idea just how on the mark she was with her comment.

Their twentieth high school reunion was certainly going to make history.

Only not in the way she imagined.

Showing off her hot new young boyfriend was soon going to take a back seat to a dead body turning up even before the class president's welcome speech was over.

Chapter 2

After leaving Sabrina and Mason, Hayley drove home, hoping that Dr. Aaron Palmer was waiting for her at her house with some lit candles, a bottle of wine, and some bubble bath for later. Their busy schedules had kept them apart for six weeks. It seemed as if every time they planned a romantic dinner, some golden retriever suffered a heat stroke or a Maltese experienced respiratory distress, and Aaron would dutifully have to race back to his pet clinic.

And it wasn't just Aaron.

Hayley was busy at work, too, especially now that the summer tourist season was getting underway after a particularly brutal cold winter and rainy spring.

But finally, after two weeks of planning, both of them had managed to carve out tonight to spend some time together.

Just the two of them.

Dustin was staying at his friend Spanky's house.

Gemma had softball practice and was going out for pizza afterward with the team.

There was no one to interrupt their carefully planned intimate evening.

So Hayley felt no guilt when she wrapped up her cocktail hour with Sabrina and her new boy toy Mason after only forty-five minutes and slapped down enough bills to cover her Jack and Coke, promising to help Sabrina finalize the plans for their reunion in any way she could as she dashed out the door.

Sabrina thanked her and told her she would be in touch.

When Hayley pulled into the driveway of her house, she saw Aaron's Honda Odyssey parked out on the street.

She had a tingling sensation as she shifted the Kia's gear into park and shut off the ignition.

Hayley was flushed with excitement.

Or at least she hoped she was flushed with excitement.

Otherwise she might be experiencing some kind of medical emergency.

Anticipating this night with Aaron was what had been getting her through the whole month.

And now, it was finally here.

When Hayley entered the kitchen through the back door, she noticed all the lights in the house were dim.

There was an open bottle of wine and two glasses on the counter.

Check.

From the living room she saw an orange light flickering in the shadows.

Candles.

Check.

And as she rounded the corner into the living room, she saw a bottle of Lollia Relax Bubble Bath wrapped with a lavender ribbon.

One of Oprah's favorite things.

And so, of course, one of Hayley's too.

So far Aaron was batting a thousand.

"Aaron?" Hayley asked, poking her head around to see if he was waiting for her on the couch, but he wasn't there.

"Aaron?"

From upstairs she heard feet shuffling and then Aaron's distinct baritone voice. "You home already?"

He pounded down the stairs in a white terry-cloth robe and carrying an empty basket but for a few stray rose petals stuck to the bottom.

Hayley looked him up and down. "What are you doing?"

"I was covering your bed with rose petals. You didn't give me a chance to finish so I just dumped the whole basket on top of the bed. It's not the aesthetic I was going for."

Hayley walked over to him and kissed him softly on the lips. "No, it's perfect."

"Really? So the odds are good I'm going to get

lucky tonight? Because I'm really hoping I get lucky tonight. It's been a while."

"Trust me. I've thought of every conceivable interruption and I have headed it off at the pass. No one is going to bother us tonight."

"Good," Aaron said, grabbing her by her butt cheeks and pulling her into him. "Because I say we skip the wine, blow out the candles and start with the bath."

"When did you become such a mind reader?" Hayley said, smiling, as she ran her fingers over Aaron's bare chest underneath the white robe.

They kissed again.

Suddenly without warning Aaron bent down and scooped Hayley up in his arms.

"Aaron, what are you doing?"

"This is my best attempt at being chivalrous. I'm going to carry you upstairs."

"Are you crazy? You'll hurt yourself."

Hayley was remembering what Sabrina had said about her second husband Jerry's back going out during an ill-fated attempt at sex. She didn't want the same fate befalling Aaron.

"Seriously. Put me down. I can walk."

"I know you can walk. But I want to carry you."

They had reached the foot of the staircase. Hayley noticed perspiration forming on Aaron's forehead, but he was trying his best to hide the gargantuan effort it was taking to lug Hayley up the stairs with a forced smile.

Up the stairs they went.

One foot after another.

On the third step, Aaron had to toss Hayley a few inches into the air with all his might to adjust his grip on her. When she came back down, the strain of her weight was almost too much, but he kept that big smile plastered on his face. He was not going to admit feeling any pain.

Why did she have to pack on seven pounds during the winter? She usually lost most of it in the spring so she would be at a good weight for the summer, but this year the April showers were more like an April biblical flood so she hadn't exercised nearly enough. She spent most of the season sitting at home watching Lifetime movies and baking cakes and pies.

Finally after what seemed like an eternity, Aaron's foot settled on the top of the landing.

They were almost home free.

Just a mere seven feet from the bathroom where the hot water was already running. Hayley could make out the steam rising from the tub and fogging the mirror.

They were going to make it.

And she promised herself she would make it worth his while.

But then she heard the back door slam open and a familiar voice scream, "Mom!"

No.

Please, God, no.

Gemma wasn't supposed to be home until nine o'clock.

It wasn't even seven.

There was thumping up the stairs.

Aaron just stood there with Hayley in his arms, not having a clue what to do.

Gemma, wearing a green and gold softball shirt, matching cap, and khaki shorts suddenly appeared, a euphoric look on her face. "You will never believe what just happened! We finished softball practice and were going out for pizza when all of a sudden I saw Nate Forte hanging around the ball field waiting to talk to me. And guess what? He asked me to prom! Can you believe it? I have been crushing on this guy all year, and I didn't even think he knew I existed, and then all of a sudden out of the blue he asks me to be his date for the prom!"

"That's wonderful, Gemma, but why aren't you out having pizza with the rest of the team *like you said you were going to?*"

"Pizza? Are you kidding me? I have to lose ten pounds!"

Like mother like daughter.

Aaron was now sweating profusely, the beads landing on his white terrycloth robe as he struggled to keep Hayley in his arms.

"Mom, did you sprain your foot or something?" Gemma asked, as if noticing the scene she had just interrupted for the first time.

"No, I . . . I mean, Aaron and I were just . . . it's . . . we . . . ." Haley stammered.

"And why is it so dark? Did you forget to pay the electric bill again?"

"We were just . . ." Aaron tried interjecting helpfully, but then didn't know where to go from there.

A lightbulb went off in Gemma's head.

"Oh, wow. I get it. Don't mind me. I'll be in my room. Just pretend I'm not here." Gemma scooted into her bedroom and slammed her door.

Aaron's knees suddenly buckled and he and Hayley fell to the floor with a thud.

"Damn, Hayley, I'm so sorry. Are you hurt?"

"Only my pride."

"You think there is any way we can salvage this evening?"

"Yes. In about an hour or so."

"Why an hour?"

"That's probably going to be how long it takes to mop up the bathroom?"

"What? Why?"

Water was gushing over the side of the tub as it overflowed.

Aaron jumped to his feet and ran in to turn off the water but slipped on the floor and landed hard on his butt.

You know what they say about the best laid plans.

Chapter 3

"You can't boycott the reunion!" Hayley wailed before stuffing a forkful of her favorite Jalapeno Macaroni and Cheese into her mouth at the Side Street Cafe. She was cramming in a quick lunch with best friends, Mona Barnes and Liddy Crawford, and Mona had just unceremoniously announced she would not be participating in their upcoming high school class reunion.

"Give me one good reason why not," Mona growled before chugging the rest of her Bar Harbor Blueberry Ale.

"Because it will give you a chance to catch up with people you haven't seen in twenty years," Hayley said.

"I see you two every week. That's enough. And I run into half our class all the friggin' time at the grocery store and at the high school basketball games. As for the rest of the uppity snobs who went to fancy colleges and got high-paying jobs and just want to come back to the island and flaunt their success in front of us, well, to hell with them!"

"You really shouldn't force her to go if she doesn't want to, Hayley," Liddy said quietly while stirring her cup of Jasmine tea with a silver spoon.

"But she *has* to go! I can name a dozen class-mates coming from all over who will be disappointed if Mona's a no show."

"And I can name twice as many more who would rather not have a repeat of our ten-year reunion," Liddy added, squeezing a lemon into her cup before delicately taking a sip.

"That *wasn't* Mona's fault," Hayley said hastily.

"Of course it wasn't my fault," Mona bellowed. "That punk ass DJ you hired from Bangor refused to play *any* music from the year we graduated! I thought that was the whole point! Was it really going to kill him to play one, just *one* Hootie and the Blowfish song?"

"You didn't have to punch him in the face!"

"I've told you a hundred times, Liddy! That was *not* my fault."

"How can you blame the DJ? He just asked you politely to back away slowly from his turntable and then you went on the attack like some feral Pit Bull that hadn't been fed in a week!"

"I don't blame the DJ. I blame *you*!"

"Me? How is your lightning quick temper *my* fault?"

"Because you were the one who insisted on splurging for an open bar, and you know how I get when I am overserved!"

"Ladies, please. Can we dial it back a bit, please? You're scaring the wait staff," Hayley begged, nodding to the bar.

A few of the servers were bunched up together, their eyes glued to the loud scene. When Mona spun her head around like Linda Blair in that *Exorcist* movie and glared at them, smoke practically steaming out of her ears, they banged into each other, pretending to be hard at work and not watching.

"Well, I'll vote to have a cash bar this year so we don't have a repeat of our tenth reunion," Hayley offered diplomatically, while poking at the last bit of macaroni in her bowl.

"I'm still not going," Mona barked.

"Why not?" Hayley asked, sighing.

"If I never lay eyes on those three mean girl bitches who made our lives a living hell in high school then I'll count myself lucky!"

"You mean Sabrina, Nykki, and Ivy? They're not so bad, Mona," Liddy said, slurping down the rest of her tea.

"Not so bad? Are you kidding me? They wrote the word *dyke* on my locker in lipstick just because I had short hair and was fond of wearing bulky sweatshirts with dirty jokes written on the front."

"You *still* have short hair and wear bulky sweatshirts with dirty jokes written on the front," Liddy said, smiling.

"Those girls were vicious. They didn't care that I had a picture of Brad Pitt barechested wearing a cowboy hat from *Thelma and Louise* taped to my locker! They just didn't like the way I dressed or acted so they made me a target! Don't get me wrong! I love lesbians. Some nights I hear my husband farting and I see my kids starting a mash potato fight and I think to myself, why on earth didn't God make me a lesbian? I'd be so much happier!"

"I think we're getting a little off track," Hayley said, scraping the bottom of her bowl for any excess clumps of cheese before setting her fork down. "I'm certainly not making excuses for them. They were horrible to me too. But that was twenty years ago. I've at least gotten to know Sabrina better through my dealings with her as county coroner and she's mellowed. I'm sure Nykki and Ivy have too. People change."

"I haven't changed," Mona said huffily.

"You can say that again," Liddy whispered under her breath.

"Liddy, you're not helping!" Hayley barked.

"I'm just saying, I'm exactly the same as I was in high school so I don't expect those high and mighty harpies to have changed either!"

"Hayley, she's not going. Accept it," Liddy said.

"Now you've got me all worked up. I need another blueberry ale before I go back out on my boat to haul traps!" Mona grumbled while waving a finger at the skittish waitresses, who cowered at the sound of her voice.

Chapter 4

Hayley scurried back to the office after hugging Liddy and Mona goodbye in the parking lot behind the Side Street Cafe. She tip-toed through the door to the *Island Times* front office and noiselessly slipped behind her desk hoping nobody would notice she had taken an extra fifteen minutes for lunch. Mostly due to Mona's ranting about the upcoming reunion.

As she set her bag on the floor next to her chair, she heard someone clear his throat and it startled her. She looked up to see a gangly, awkward kid with a pronounced nose and big brown puppy dog eyes, around seventeen years old, slumped in a chair across from her and holding a large brown paper bag.

"Hi, Mrs. Powell," the boy said, his voice cracking.

"I'm sorry, and you are . . . ?" Hayley said, sizing the kid up, trying to place him, but having no luck.

"Oliver Whitfield," he said, offering a stiff smile. "I'm in your daughter Gemma's class."

"Why aren't you in school, Oliver?"

"Oh, the principal lets me off at one on Tuesdays and Thursdays to help out at my parents' new sandwich shop. It's like a work-study program. I'm learning the business and even help out with the books. But my Dad's sick today so I'm handling deliveries."

Hayley remembered seeing an ad for a new sandwich shop in town called Well Bread. She had heard a new family called the Whitfields had recently moved to Bar Harbor from Ohio, but she hadn't met them yet.

"Well, it's nice to meet you, Oliver. Did somebody here at the office order some sandwiches?"

Oliver nodded.

"Does anybody back there know you're here?"

Oliver shook his head.

"How long have you been sitting here?"

"About fifteen minutes. Nobody was here and I didn't want to bother anybody so I thought I'd just wait."

"I see. Well, there's no point in mentioning that to anyone, especially my boss, so let's pretend you just walked through the door. It's not like the sandwiches had time to get soggy, right?"

Oliver nodded again.

"Who placed the order? I'll have them come out and pay you."

"Mr. Linney."

Bruce Linney.

The *Island Times* crime reporter.

And a big pain in the you know what.

"Mrs. Powell, I'm glad I ran into you because I wanted to ask—"

Before the kid could finish his sentence, Hayley's corpulent boss, Editor-in-Chief Sal Moretti, stormed out from the back bullpen and roared at the top of his lungs, "What the hell took you so long, kid? My stomach's growling so loud I can't hear myself think!"

"Sorry, sir," Oliver said meekly.

Sal yanked the brown paper bag out of the kid's bony little fingers and stuffed his hammy fist in it, pulling out a giant-size sandwich wrapped in white paper. "This my roast beef with cheddar cheese and horse radish?"

Oliver nodded.

"Great. Bruce is in his office on the phone. He'll be right out to take care of the bill."

"Sal, didn't you already have lunch? I saw you leave around 11:30 with some of your fishing buddies to go have fried clams at the Thirsty Whale."

The moment the words came tumbling out she regretted saying them.

"Yeah, okay, I had an early lunch. Before noon. It's after two now. Can't a guy have a midday snack? What are you all of a sudden, the food police? I'm hungry! Sue me!"

"You're absolutely right. You work hard. You deserve a little afternoon treat," Hayley said, backpedaling.

Sal had already unwrapped the sandwich and

taken a giant bite. A few strands of stray roast beef hung out of the side of his mouth, bouncing up and down in front of his bottom lip as he chewed.

Both Hayley and Oliver pretended not to notice.

"So Mrs. Powell, while I'm here there's something I'd like to—"

"Well, well, well, look who's finally back from lunch," Bruce Linney sneered as he sailed into the front office and snatched the brown paper bag off Hayley's desk where Sal had set it down to free both of his pudgy hands so he could devour the stack of roast beef and cheese between the two pieces of homemade rye bread.

"You got my turkey avocado, kid?"

"Yes, sir. With extra mayo."

"Right," Bruce said, slightly embarrassed. "Don't worry. I ran two miles this morning before work."

But nobody in the office really cared about how much mayo Bruce was consuming even though his ego would forcefully disagree.

Bruce plucked a twenty dollar bill out of his wallet and handed it to Oliver. "That should cover it and leave you a little extra for a tip."

"Actually, sir, it's twenty-one dollars and sixty-two cents."

"That's awfully pricey for a couple of sandwiches, if you ask me," Bruce said with a raised eyebrow.

"That includes your sandwich from yesterday which you didn't pay for yet. You said to start a tab. But my Dad really wants me to collect today."

"Oh. Okay. Hayley, can you cover it with petty cash? I promise to replace it tomorrow. It's just that I've been working through lunch lately and staying late because I've been so busy I haven't had a moment to go to the ATM or take care of any of life's little errands."

"Was that for my benefit, Bruce? You know how much I hate a kiss ass!" Sal yelled, his mouth full, chewed up pieces of bread and meat flying across the office like Japanese Kamikazes.

Bruce was speechless as Sal wandered back to his office. After quickly unfolding the white wrapping paper to insure the sandwich shop had prepared his turkey avocado to his exact specifications, Bruce followed, leaving Hayley alone with Oliver.

Hayley had already counted out some dollar bills to cover the rest of the bill as well as a generous tip for the delivery boy.

Oliver smiled as he pocketed the money and then pulled out a small plastic bag filled with gourmet potato chips and handed it to Hayley.

"What's this?"

"I brought them special just for you."

"Me? Why that's so thoughtful, Oliver. Thank you."

"I knew you would be working today."

"Well, I will be sure to try them later. I just came back from lunch and I'm quite full at the moment."

"They're homemade. My mother makes a bunch of different flavors. This one is Gorgonzola Red Onion."

That was all Hayley needed to hear.

She ripped open the bag and tried one.

"Oh my God, these are so decadently delicious."

She tried another.

And another.

And another.

What was that saying about not being able to stop after just one?

"So I was wondering if you could tell me . . ." Oliver said, his voice trailing off as if he was debating whether or not to ask.

"What is it, Oliver?"

"Do you know if . . . um . . . well I was hoping you might . . ."

"Sometimes it's best just to spit it out."

"Does Gemma have a date for senior prom?"

This was not what Hayley was expecting.

"Actually, just last night Gemma told me she had been asked by a boy named Nate Forte," Hayley said, feeling sorry for the kid who suddenly looked crestfallen.

"I see. Well, I'm not surprised. She's a very popular girl and . . ."

His voice trailed off again.

"But I'm sure she will be flattered you asked," Hayley said, knowing full well this would not make the poor boy feel any better.

"Yeah, I better go," Oliver said softly before beating a hasty retreat.

"Thank you for the chips," Hayley managed to get out before the door slammed behind him.

Sal stomped out of his office. "Hayley, check the bag to see if my side of chips is in there."

Sal stopped suddenly at the sight of Hayley's hand inside the now half eaten plastic bag of homemade potato chips Oliver had so kindly presented to her. She instantly dropped the chips on her desk and rummaged through the brown paper bag but there were no other bags of chips.

"The boy told me he brought them special for me. I didn't know you had ordered a side of chips, Sal, I swear!"

"Isn't it convenient the kid is long gone and not here to back up your flimsy story!" Sal said, folding his fat arms and glaring at her.

Hayley picked up the bag and tried to hand what was left of the chips to Sal. "You can have the rest of them if you want."

"After your wet fingers have been all over them? You know I won't even share a tub of popcorn with my own wife at the movies! I hate people's fingers being on my food!"

"I'm sorry. Listen, I should probably wait until you've cooled down a bit before I ask about some time off . . ."

"Really? You want to ask for time off *now*? After you've inhaled most of *my* potato chips? Is that what you really want to do?"

"It's just that my high school reunion is coming up, and I promised to help plan the whole thing, not to mention Gemma's prom and I have to take her dress shopping . . ."

"You're talking to me like I care about any of this. You know June is our busy season. Tourists are pouring in from all over and we have to cover a lot of stories and I'm understaffed as it is . . ."

"I do have a few personal days and a couple of

vacation days left that I could cobble together. I'd be out for a week tops . . ."

"I see your lips moving but I'm not hearing what you're saying."

"Sal, please. What if I ran to the sandwich shop right now and brought you back three bags of potato chips, each one a different flavor?"

"I'm listening."

"And paid for it out of my own money! Not petty cash."

"I'm still listening."

"And I hear they also sell these amazing peanut butter cookies."

"One week, Hayley. But you get no break from your column. You don't have to come into the office, but you still have to make your deadlines! If one column is late, it's right back in the office. No excuses."

"It's a deal."

"Now go get me my chips," Sal said, wiping a small glob of horseradish off the corner of his mouth with his bare knuckle and licking it off.

Hayley was out the door in a flash.

Island Food & Spirits
by
Hayley Powell

With my daughter's senior prom looming right around the corner, the quest to find the perfect dress became the top priority in our household.

So when I arrived home one night last week exhausted from a long day at the office, all I wanted to do was make myself a cocktail, kick back, and relax. I had a taste for something cold and refreshing. A delicious creamy concoction called a Dreamsicle. So I had picked up the ingredients on the way home.

As I entered the house through the back door with my recyclable grocery bag, I stopped suddenly at the chaotic disaster that was my kitchen.

For a brief moment as I stood there in stunned silence surveying the mess, I thought I had stumbled into one of those crime scene investigation rooms that they set up after a murder occurs, just like the ones on *Criminal Minds,* of which I am a loyal viewer. I have a raging crush on that dashing Joe Mantegna, and of course the hunky Shemar Moore. Hell, I love all the men on that show. But I digress. Let's get back to the state of my kitchen. There were rows and rows of pictures tacked up on the wall like murder victims and suspects.

Upon closer inspection, I realized the pictures were of models wearing various party gowns and designer couture. On the floor were four teenage girls surrounded by piles of magazines and armed with scissors as they furiously cut out every photo of a dress they could find. In the hallway were stacks of ripped up and shredded magazines that they had already meticulously pored through.

The girls hadn't noticed me yet.

"What do you think you're doing?" I demanded to know.

In hindsight, I probably should have opened and shut the door again or even just cleared my throat to alert them to my presence, but I guess that's why they call it hindsight.

My booming voice startled the girls so much they erupted in screams and one was so frightened she threw her scissors. I had to duck to avoid losing my right eye.

That's when I noticed the giant pile of discarded magazines in the hallway just outside the kitchen begin to move and come to life. Apparently the screaming awoke my dog, Leroy, who was sleeping underneath the magazines. He shot out of the giant pile like his tail was on fire, totally confused and sliding all over the floor on the slippery papers while trying to find his footing.

My daughter berated me for scaring them as her traumatized friend sputtered apologies for nearly stabbing me in the face. I gave the girls five minutes to clean up my kitchen and then whipped up my yummy Dreamsicle cocktail, leaving them alone while I plopped down in my favorite chair with Leroy snuggling next to me, and then surfed the channels until I found a *Criminal Minds* rerun.

Studly Shemar was chasing down a suspect, which normally would keep me glued to the TV, but all the prom dress talk and visuals in my kitchen brought up a feeling of nostalgia, so I ran to a drawer in my den and hauled out my old photo album from senior year. I flipped through it until I found a picture of me in my prom dress. My curly brown hair piled high on my head. My too-fake tan from a can. A wide smile plastered on my face. You could tell I thought my dress was the fashion statement of the century. It was a strapless gown that was fitted to the waist. From the waist on down was layers upon layers of what seemed like floating chiffon that stopped just above my knees. The color of the dress was a bright over-the-top orange. Same color as my Dreamsicle cocktail! Of course! All this talk about prom and dresses must have subconsciously brought back the memory of my own dress and the color triggered my craving for a Dreamsicle cocktail!

Now that I had almost downed the entire cocktail, maybe it was time for something more substantial. Once the girls cleared out of the kitchen, maybe I had the ingredients to bake a Dreamy Orange Dreamsicle Cake!

* * *

Dreamsicle Cocktail

Ingredients:

2 ounces vanilla vodka
2 ounces cream
4 ounces orange juice
1 ounce triple sec

Fill your shaker with ice half way (chill beforehand if you have time) then add in all of your ingredients. Shake vigorously, then pour into a tall cocktail glass with ice, then sip and you will feel just like a kid again!

Dreamy Orange Dreamsicle Cake

Ingredients:

1 box orange cake mix
2 eggs
½ cup oil
1½ cups water
3 ounce box of orange Jell-O mix

Preheat your oven to 350 degrees. Then combine all of your ingredients in a bowl and with an electric mixer mix for 2 minutes until blended.

Pour into a greased and floured 13x9 baking dish.

Bake for 30 minutes or until a toothpick inserted in the middle comes out clean.

Cool your cake completely then frost with a whipped topping of your choice.

Chapter 5

Hayley and Liddy had been waiting thirty-five minutes for their classmates, Sabrina Merryweather, Nykki Temple, and Ivy Foster, who were the self-appointed high school reunion planning committee. They had all agreed to meet at the reunion venue, the Kebo Valley Golf Club, precisely at 4:00 PM. It was no shocker the mean girls were late. Ever since high school it was assumed (by them) that their time was always more valuable than anybody else's.

Liddy was steaming and ready to wash her hands of the whole affair and drive home, but Hayley stalled her by soliciting her ideas for how they should handle the reunion. Liddy loved to be consulted on how to plan an event, but when it came down to the nitty gritty details and the actual hard work of seeing it through, her interest quickly waned.

Liddy still couldn't believe the mean girls had put off planning the reunion until just a few days before, so she strongly believed the best course of action was to go simple. Nothing too fancy.

"I can call in a few favors. There's that new caterer, Betsy Myers, who just moved to town. She does a delicious assortment of appetizers and I'm certain she'll give us a break because I got her a great deal on her house."

"Well, I'm just happy that the cooking won't be my responsibility for once," Hayley said.

"We'll do a cash bar to save money and Sonny loves to DJ on the side so I'm sure he'd be willing to spin tunes for free if I ask nicely."

Sonny Lipton was a local baby-faced lawyer and Liddy's current beau who was a good deal younger than her.

"And if that doesn't work, I can always use other means of persuasions," Liddy said, cocking her head to the side and winking at Hayley.

"Enough! I don't need to hear the details," Hayley said, putting a hand up.

"Anyway, I've crunched the numbers and I think if we really went bare bones we could get away with just charging twenty dollars per person."

"What about decorations?"

"We're adults celebrating twenty long years since high school. We're way past the crepe paper and streamers stage. The golf club looks lovely just the way it is. This is more about seeing old faces than over-the-top decorations."

That sounded good to Hayley, who stared out

the bay windows overlooking the lush green golf course.

This place was perfect.

At that moment, the door to the main dining room and bar, which served as the nineteenth hole for club members, swung open and in breezed Sabrina along with one of her foot soldiers from high school, Nykki Temple.

Nykki was still a spark plug. Short. Fiery red hair. And wearing a casual business suit that was almost an exact replica of the one Liddy was wearing.

And Hayley knew that was not lost on the extremely style conscious Liddy Crawford, whose eyes nearly popped out of her head.

Nykki kept her distance, acknowledging Hayley with a slight wave as her eyes stayed glued to her smart phone.

"I'm so sorry we're late," Nykki said in a clipped voice that betrayed not a hint of remorse. "It's all my fault. Sabrina and I decided to car pool but when she showed up at the hotel to pick me up I was still out showing a lovely home with ten acres of land just outside of town to an interested couple from Delaware looking for a summer getaway."

"I . . . I beg your pardon . . . ?" Liddy stammered, not quite believing her ears. "What are you doing showing property in Maine? Don't you live in Boston?"

"Yes. But I have my real estate license in every

state in New England," Nykki said, not even making eye contact with Liddy. "The thing is, I found a summer rental in Seal Harbor on the water for me, Ivy and her husband, and Sabrina and her boyfriend to share. Four bedrooms. Classic New England style. Steps from the ocean. It got me thinking. I could clean up here. I'm bored selling high-end condos in Boston. Maybe it's time to pull up stakes and move home again."

"You do realize I am the premier real estate agent on Mount Desert Island," Liddy said, clenching her fists so tight her knuckles turned white.

"Oh yes," Nykki said, finally looking up from her phone, a sly smile on her face.

"But why would you want to move back *here*? You must remember the awful rough winters and the messy muddy springs not to mention the slim pickings when it comes to finding a man. I can tell you're still single because you're not wearing a wedding ring and let's face it, Hayley snapped up the last good one to come to town, Dr. Aaron, a hot veterinarian."

"Bravo for you, Hayley," Nykki said. "But I'm not looking for a husband thank you very much."

Liddy was now on an emotional spiral.

The last thing she needed was increased competition in the local real estate game.

Hayley stepped forward and gently touched her arm. She knew her friend would be completely useless for the rest of the planning committee meeting.

But before Hayley had a chance to pitch their low-cost ideas for the reunion, the door swung open again and Sabrina's other wingman, Ivy Foster, walked, or rather, danced inside. Ivy, with her flowing curly blond hair, and flower child essence, was more of a let-it-all-hang-out girl, wearing a loose sun dress with a green print that looked suspiciously like marijuana plants. She squealed in delight and grabbed Hayley in a bear hug, squeezing her so tight, as if they had actually been close in high school.

As Ivy descended upon Liddy, she tried to back away, a panicked look in her eye, but there was no escaping Ivy, who succeeded in wrapping her bony arms around her as Liddy wiggled to free herself.

Luckily for Liddy, the moment was broken by a cacophony of barking.

Or rather yapping.

Loud, intense, ear-splitting yapping.

Seven scampering high-energy toy poodles strained at their leashes to wreck havoc in the golf club held back only by a bespectacled wavy haired wisp of a man in a bright yellow golf shirt and green pants, his large hands attached to frighteningly skinny arms trying valiantly to keep a hold on the seven leashes.

Ivy was completely oblivious to the storm of activity in her wake. She just simply talked above the noise. "Oh my God, Hayley and Liddy, you two haven't changed a bit! You look just like you did in high school!"

A backhanded compliment to be sure since Hayley fought acne and frizzy hair right up to high school graduation and beyond.

"You have to meet my family," Ivy cooed.

But instead of introducing her husband, she began rattling off the names of her miniature dogs he was desperately trying to corral. "This is Doc. Sleepy. Happy. Grumpy. Sneezy. Bashful. Dopey."

Hayley had seen *Snow White and the Seven Dwarfs* enough times with her kids to know the dogs were wearing knitted sweaters that matched in color the costumes of their namesakes from the 1937 animated classic.

Someone was a true Disneyphile.

"They're my babies!" Ivy shouted over the din of her barking dogs. "I never go anywhere without them."

"I can't believe there's only seven of them," Liddy yelled. "Sounds more like *101 Dalmatians.*"

"Oh, I loved that movie too!" Ivy screamed, choosing to ignore the true intent of Liddy's remark. "I love anything Disney. We have an annual pass to the theme park. We fly to Orlando every vacation."

"Hello, everyone," her husband said in a thick British accent, almost out of breath from wrestling with the tiny dogs, "I'm another person in the room."

"Oh, right. This is my husband Nigel. If I knew

how sarcastic the English were, I probably never would have said, 'I do.'"

"We all have our regrets in life, to be sure," Nigel said icily.

The tension was thick in the room, broken only by the still barking dogs.

Hayley quickly stepped forward and shook his hand. "Nice to meet you, Nigel. I'm Hayley. Did you two bond over your love of everything Disney?"

"Good God no!" Nigel spit out. "I pray every night the factory where they mass produce those tacky little porcelain figurines based on every character in every cartoon they've ever made would burn to the ground in a raging fire so I wouldn't have to find room in our house on some shelf or nightstand or coffee table every time they put a damn movie out."

Ivy reached down and picked up one of her dogs. "This isn't the only one we call Grumpy."

Suddenly one of the dogs, Sneezy if Hayley had kept track of the names correctly, spotted a squirrel sprinting across a tree branch just outside the window of the dining room, and led a revolt. He wrenched free from Nigel's grasp, surprising him and causing him to let go of the other six leather handles. All seven yapping dogs scratched the hardwood floors with their toenails as they raced to the window, jumping up and down, barking at the top of their lungs, trying to get to the squirrel, who was now frozen in fear and staring through the glass at them.

"Nigel, would you please take the dogs for a walk so I can have a civilized meeting with my girl-friends about the reunion?" Ivy yelled scornfully.

"But I'm supposed to play a round of golf with a nice gentleman I met in town earlier today," Nigel whined.

"I don't care. Stop being so selfish," Ivy said, before spinning around and sighing to Hayley and Liddy. "He's never willing to help me with anything! And you would think that might be his top priority since he is a struggling novelist who hasn't written anything that's sold. I'm basically supporting the two of us plus the dogs with my thriving cupcake business. Did you know I was recently featured in the pages of *Bon Appetit* magazine?"

"Congratulations," Hayley said, keeping one eye on Nigel, who had retrieved four out of the seven leashes, his face red with embarrassment over his wife berating him in front of her friends.

"I know exactly what you're going through. My ex-husband was a starving artist," Sabrina said, piling on poor Nigel. "He hardly touched a brush to his canvas because he was more interested in watching cable news and leaving *me* to pay all the bills!"

Nigel at this point looked completely emasculated, wanting to disappear into the floor.

Hayley attempted to break the tension. "What kind of books do you write, Nigel?"

"Murder mysteries!" Nigel bellowed, snapping up the last of the leashes and yanking the dogs back from the window so aggressively they all slammed into one another.

"I love murder mysteries! Are you writing one now?" Hayley hollered over the high pitched yelping.

"Yes. I'm working on a story about a henpecked husband who murders his nagging wife! But the twist ending is he gets away with it because after hearing the torture she put him through, the jury refuses to convict him!"

There was an awkward silence.

Except for the barking dogs.

Without saying another word, Nigel wrangled the leashes and stormed out, dragging the dogs behind him.

Finally there was quiet.

"Let's get started, shall we?" Sabrina said, with a fake smile on her face to cover the fact she had just witnessed such an uncomfortable domestic drama.

"Well, Liddy and I had a chance to talk before you got here . . ." Hayley said.

"Since you were all so late," Liddy barked, almost as piercing as Ivy's dogs.

Hayley quickly brushed past the comment. "Anyway, we think since time is such an issue we should just keep things simple and not go overboard because, after all, the whole point of the reunion is to just reconnect with old friends and catch up after so many years apart, right?"

Sabrina, Nykki, and Ivy exchanged glances

before Nykki motioned for Sabrina to speak on their behalf.

"Hayley, we appreciate you and Liddy taking the initiative and trying to make our lives easier but this reunion, it's not like the tenth, when we were still kids, finding our way in life. This is the big one. Twenty years. We've all accomplished so much in life. Well, a few of us anyway. Why treat it just like any other run of the mill cocktail party?"

"We should go big. Have a live band. Maybe a singer or group who were really popular the year we graduated," Nykki said to nods of approval from Sabrina and Ivy.

"Yes! Like Seal or Mariah Carey!" Sabrina said, clapping her hands.

"Or Tupac!"

"He's dead, Ivy," Liddy said, scowling.

"Oh. Okay. Well, then maybe we can also get a celebrity from that era to give some kind of welcome speech. I may have an in with Jason Priestly."

"Oh my God! Maybe Luke Perry could also come and they could be like co-speakers! That would be so fabulous!" Sabrina added, excited about their spitballing.

Liddy stared at them, skepticism written all over her face. "With three days notice?"

"You know, Liddy," Nykki said pointedly. "Maybe if you weren't so negative you'd sell more houses. A positive attitude is the key to success."

For a moment, Hayley thought she was going

to have to tackle Liddy who looked like she was about to lunge at Nykki and physically assault her.

But surprisingly Liddy showed remarkable restraint.

Although she did look like she was about to cry.

"And decorations! We should recreate that simpler time in our lives. With lots of crepe paper and streamers," Sabrina said to nods of approval from Ivy. "Really dress up this rather staid and architecturally outdated golf club."

As Hayley and Liddy watched the three former mean girls chatter away about their big ideas, it was very clear they had officially been pushed out of the planning.

Nykki suddenly held a finger up for silence as she read a text on her phone. "Girls, I have to adjourn this meeting for now because I just got a last-minute showing out in Town Hill. A couple wants to take a look on their way out of town so it has to be now or never. They're already there waiting."

"But Nykki, I have to pick up Mason at the rental house because we're going on a sunset cruise with Patty Simcox from high school who married one of the Rockefellers," Sabrina said frowning.

"I have an idea," Ivy said. "Sabrina can drop me off at the house when she picks up Mason and you can just take my rental car, Nykki."

"Works for me," Sabrina said.

"Perfect. You're a doll, Ivy," Nykki said. "I think

this was all incredibly productive. Let's reconnoiter later tonight and dole out specific tasks."

As the three of them hustled for the door, Hayley called after them. "Wait. What about Nigel? He's still out walking the dogs."

"Oh, don't worry about him," Ivy said, rolling her eyes. "He can walk home."

"But your rental is like seven miles outside of town."

That didn't really seem to be an issue with Ivy.

"Okay. Well, don't worry," Hayley said. "Liddy and I can just wait here and give him a lift back to the rental house when he gets back."

"Absolutely not," Ivy said, shaking her head. "Nigel's getting fat around the middle, it's like he's wearing a Michelin tire. He needs the exercise so don't you dare!"

It was clear to Hayley that she was no longer on the receiving end of Ivy's cruel streak like she was in high school.

The new target was her husband.

Chapter 6

"You know, seeing Nykki and Ivy reunited with their queen bee Sabrina after all these years wasn't really what I expected," Liddy said, gripping the wheel of her Mercedes as she drove Hayley home.

"Not as bad as you thought?"

"No. Worse!"

"Oh, come on, Liddy. I think it's safe to say they've all mellowed just a little bit," Hayley said, not really believing her own words.

"Were you in the same room as I was?" Liddy asked incredulously as she whipped her head around to look at Hayley.

"Keep your eyes on the road!" Hayley yelled as she watched the Mercedes slowly drift over the yellow center dividing line into the opposite lane.

Liddy jerked the wheel back to the left and shook her head. "Once a nasty bitch always a nasty bitch. If that walking demon seed Nykki thinks she's going to encroach on *my* territory, I will fight her to the death!"

"You have to admit, Sabrina has calmed down a lot since high school. I mean, she's been through two painful divorces, and since leaving her job as county coroner, she's definitely not as manic and career obsessed."

"Why are you cutting her so much slack?"

"Because it's not healthy to hold a grudge. I'm practicing forgiveness."

"Well, stop it! It's irritating! Have you forgotten how they treated you in high school? How awful they were to you?"

"Of course not. But it's been twenty years. I think it's time to let all that go and just put it behind me."

"They despised Mona and me but mostly ignored us. Which was fine by us. But you, they especially had it out for you. At least with us, they didn't pretend to like us. They'd string you along and make you believe you were part of their clique and then without warning they'd just freeze you out and make you feel like nothing!"

"What part of putting this behind me didn't resonate with you?"

"Remember that night the summer after graduation? It was the weekend after Fourth of July and Mona went on a fishing trip with her Dad and I flew to New York with my mother to meet my college roommate in the fall, and you were left to your own devices and once again fell into their trap?"

Hayley did remember.

In fact, it was impossible to forget.

July 1995.

Hayley stood in front of the bathroom mirror staring at the unsightly pimple hovering just above her upper lip.

Maybe it was a cold sore she got from making out with Mark Peterman during Senior Skip Day.

Oh God.

Why isn't it going away?

She resisted the urge to pop it.

Her dermatologist forbade her to ever try ridding her face of a zit using that method. He warned her it would only grow back. Twice the size as before. Maybe he was just trying to scare her.

She was about to turn eighteen.

How could she still be fighting such an adolescent malady as acne?

Of all nights to be sporting a big fat ugly white pimple.

Sabrina Merryweather had invited her over for a party. Her parents were away on business, and she had secured a keg from her college-age brother and was inviting a few of her closest girlfriends along with an impressive selection of boys for an intimate party in her backyard.

And looking back at her through the mirror was Quasimoto's frizzy-haired gawky younger sister.

She couldn't go.

Not looking like this.

She had already lied to her mother and told her it was an innocent slumber party. They were going to the Criterion Theatre to see that new Alicia Silverstone movie Clueless. *It was supposed to be a hoot. But that was just the cover story. No boys were interested in seeing a romantic comedy loosely based on a Jane Austen novel.*

Why did she have to lie anyway?

She was on the verge of adulthood.

But as long as she was under her mother's roof, she had to follow her annoying rules. Hence the elaborate girls' movie night and slumber party yarn.

She had gone to so much trouble concocting the fake scenario; she couldn't bow out of the real one now. And Sabrina seemed so happy when she told her she would come. Graduation had seemed to melt away the friction between them. Hayley wasn't actually certain what had caused their rift that began sophomore year, but she was relieved it was finally coming to an end.

They had been best friends in grade school. Slumber parties at each other's houses. Science partners in eighth grade. Sat together on the school bus and shared math notes. But when they reached high school, Hayley had felt Sabrina pulling away by Christmas of freshman year. By sophomore year, the mean girl cliques took root and that's when Sabrina officially froze her out, sacrificed their years long friendship in order to secure her own place with the "in crowd", the fashion conscious, backbiting, ostracizing, rumor spreading, name-calling girls who stick together in order to feel a sense of security, a sense of identity, a sense of superiority. Sabrina had always been insecure for as long as Hayley could remember and she craved that kind of acceptance, and she was willing to do whatever it took to become one of them—even if it meant losing Hayley as her most trusted friend. It devastated Hayley, and it took her a long time to trust again. But now as their high school years were coming to a close,

Sabrina seemed to be holding out an olive branch with this invitation. Maybe she wanted bygones to be bygones.

No, she couldn't disappoint Sabrina and be a no show.

She would just have to live with the zit.

Her mother was out shopping at the grocery store so it was now or never. She slipped past her younger brother, Randy, who was stretched out on the couch watching Hercules: The Legendary Journeys *(she would later learn he was more interested in star Kevin Sorbo's biceps than the rip-roaring sword fighting action sequences). He never even noticed her leaving.*

It was a short walk to Sabrina's house and it was getting dark by the time she arrived. The lights were off in the house.

She rang the bell.

No answer.

She rang it again.

She stood outside five minutes.

Then it was ten.

Twenty.

Thirty.

She sat down on the steps, folded her hands, and checked the zit on her face.

It was still there.

After two hours, it slowly dawned on her that Sabrina wasn't coming home.

And there was no party.

Hayley dreaded going back to her house on Snow Street.

Her mother would be full of questions.

Where was Sabrina?

Why didn't she call if she needed to cancel?

Should I call her parents?

Hayley was embarrassed.

Humiliated.

She knew deep down that Sabrina and her gal pals Nykki and Ivy had probably just gotten a better offer.

And whatever it was, they weren't about to include her.

Hayley went to a pizza joint on Cottage Street teeming with tourists and had a pepperoni slice and a Diet Coke by herself before walking home while fighting back tears.

Sabrina never bothered to call the next day to explain what happened.

In fact, it was two whole weeks before Hayley ran into her on the street.

Sabrina stammered some half-assed apology.

She looked haggard and upset like she hadn't slept in weeks.

She looked terrible.

That at least made Hayley feel a little better.

And though she wanted to ask Sabrina why she and her friends had so cruelly stood her up, why she didn't even warrant a phone call to let her know the party was canceled, she just shrugged it off and continued on her way.

She wasn't the least bit interested.

She was done trying to be friends with Sabrina and her Teenage Witches.

Hayley's chirping cell phone snapped her out of the memory.

She checked the caller ID.

"It's Ivy," Hayley said.

"Don't answer it!" Liddy said, turning onto Hayley's street so fast Hayley nearly banged her head on the passenger side window despite the seat belt restraining her.

Hayley pressed the answer button and held the phone to her ear. "Hello, Ivy."

"Hi, Hayley. Listen, I called my caterer while Sabrina was driving me home and she tried gouging me with her price. I mean, come on, I like a good stuffed mushroom, but I'm not going to take out a second mortgage just to try one. If we pay her what she wants, we'd have to charge a hundred bucks a head. Now I know that doesn't mean much to you and me . . ."

Says who?

"But we really should think about our classmates who aren't doing as well as we are. They can't pay that and it would be unfair to shut them out of the reunion, don't you agree?"

"Of course, Ivy. That's sweet of you to consider them," Hayley said, pretending to gag herself with her finger.

"I don't even want to know what she's saying," Liddy growled. "What's she saying?"

Hayley shushed her.

"So after talking it over with Sabrina, we've decided to downsize. At least when it comes to the food."

"I think downsizing is an excellent idea, Ivy."

"Like we already suggested?" Liddy screamed,

craning her neck closer to the phone so Ivy could hear her.

If she did, Ivy chose to ignore it. "I'm going to make my world famous cupcakes. I think they'll put everyone in a festive mood. And don't worry. I'll pay for the ingredients myself and not charge for my time."

"That's very generous. And if there's anything I can do . . ."

"Well, since you volunteered . . ."

Why?

Why did she say anything?

She knew what was coming.

"I've read your column. You are apparently the Queen of Party Treats. So if you wouldn't mind whipping up a few appetizers. Keep in mind we have a hundred and fifty in our class, most with spouses, so I wouldn't prepare anything for less than three hundred. Thanks, Hayley. You're a peach!"

Before Hayley could protest, the line went dead.

So much for sitting on the sidelines and letting the mean girls do the heavy lifting.

Chapter 7

Hayley thought recruiting Liddy and Mona to help her prepare appetizers for the reunion would lighten the workload if they adopted an assembly line system in her kitchen, but after two bottles of BV red wine were quickly consumed within the first hour of their gal pal cooking night, the responsibility of preparing the jalapeno mozzarella sticks and the salami and cream cheese roll-ups was pretty much left to Hayley.

But Hayley wasn't complaining. At the very least, she was grateful for the moral support after being strong-armed into single-handedly catering the reunion with the exception of Ivy's self-proclaimed world famous cupcakes.

Mona teetered on top of a stool next to the small kitchen high table as she struggled to open a third bottle of wine while Liddy was still railing against Nykki Temple threatening her livelihood.

"I swear if she tries to steal one client away from me, just one, I will take her down," Liddy slurred,

waving her wine glass around and coming danger-
ously close to dousing Mona with the little bit of
Cabernet swishing around in the bottom that she
had yet to slurp down.

"Should I make those delicious parmesan garlic
chicken wings I served at last summer's Fourth of
July barbecue?" Hayley asked, opening her fridge
to inspect its contents for the right ingredients. "I
think I have some frozen wings in the freezer out
in the garage."

"Are you even listening to me?" Liddy wailed.

"Never. So why start now?" Mona chuckled as
she finally popped the cork on a fresh bottle,
nearly toppling off the stool in the process.

"Liddy, you have plenty of competition and
you've still done incredibly well for yourself. I
don't think Nykki moving back here is going to
affect your business one bit," Hayley said, stacking
the roll-ups in rows between wax paper and sliding the platter on the top shelf in her fridge.

Mona jumped down from her stool and
reached for one before Hayley had a chance to
close the refrigerator door. Hayley gently slapped
Mona on the wrist and blocked her with her body
before she had the chance to grab one. "Oh no
you don't. You only get to try them if you promise
to come to the reunion."

"Not happening," Mona said defiantly before
turning back to the bottle of wine on the counter she
had just opened and pouring some into her glass.

"Don't you have one fond memory of high
school, Mona?"

"Yeah. Graduating," Mona barked.

"Just barely, as I recall," Liddy said before grabbing the bottle away from Mona and filling her own glass.

The back door swung open and Gemma breezed in, as if walking on air. She had a dopey grin on her face, but before Hayley could ask why she looked so euphoric, she noticed a tall boy around Gemma's age following behind her. He was strikingly handsome. Hollywood handsome. Like one of those pin up boys from a CW show about sexy teen vampires or hot young ghost hunters. Blond. Built. And a megawatt smile that took your breath away.

"Mom, this is Nate. Nate Forte. We're going to prom together," Gemma cooed before catching herself and trying to strike a cooler, less overly excited girlish pose.

"Nice to meet you, Mrs. Powell," Nate said, extending a massive hand and squeezing Hayley's so tight it almost hurt.

"It's a pleasure, Nate."

"And these are my honorary aunts, Liddy and Mona," Gemma said, staring at the empty wine bottles and silently imploring them not to embarrass her.

To Liddy and Mona's credit, they simply waved at Nate and offered perfunctory smiles.

"Thanks for walking me home," Gemma said. "I'll e-mail you the history notes later so we can study together tomorrow before the final."

"Great. I'm going to need all the help I can

get," Nate said, smiling again so brightly, Hayley half expected a power outage from him sucking up so much electricity in one facial expression. "Nice meeting you all."

Hayley noticed him start to lean in to kiss Gemma, but then think better of it with her mother watching.

Instead, he patted her gently on the cheek and was out the door in a flash.

"Too bad you couldn't have scrounged up a better looking prom date, Gemma," Liddy said, watching him dash up the street from the kitchen window.

"I totally scored. Every girl in my class was vying to go with him. I have no idea why he chose me!"

"Because you're beautiful, smart, kind, funny, and my daughter," Hayley said. "There was no way he could do better."

"I hated prom," Mona said, climbing back up on the stool she was using as a perch.

"That's because you hated wearing a dress," Hayley said, laughing.

"Yeah, there was that. My mother forced me to buy one at JC Penney. Remember? It was bright yellow. I looked like Big Bird," Mona said, shaking her head.

"You went with Norman Langford, right? I remember he loved your dress. He kept complimenting it all night," Liddy said. "Frankly I think he wished he had been the one wearing it."

"Whatever happened to Norman?" Hayley asked.

"He runs a dance company in Rhode Island," Mona said.

"That sounds about right," Liddy said, nodding.

"Speaking of dresses . . ." Hayley said, turning to Gemma. "How about a sneak preview for Liddy and Mona?"

Liddy clapped her hands together, excited over the prospect of an impromptu fashion show.

Gemma demurred but it was mostly for show. It didn't take a lot of convincing before she raced up the stairs to her room to pull the dress off the hanger.

"I know she's going to have a night to remember," Hayley said. "And it has to be better than my own prom night."

"Didn't you go with Ruben Fitch?"

"Yeah, I was going through my bad boy period and Ruben fit the bill. He was just back from a three-week suspension for joyriding in his father's truck on school property and tearing up the football field. At the time, I thought his rebellious spirit was cool. But I paid the price for it. After the prom, he was arrested for public intoxication and left me to walk home in my prom dress in the rain. Then I spent the rest of the night hearing 'I told you so' from my mother. Not the happiest of memories."

Gemma descended the stairs in a Princess Sweetheart beaded sleeveless floor-length tulle dress. Even with no make-up and her hair pulled back in a lifeless pony tail, she looked absolutely stunning. Just the sight of her looking so regal and gorgeous, filling out the dress so perfectly, brought tears to Hayley's eyes.

"You look so grown up. It's killing me," Hayley said, grabbing a napkin to dab her tear-streaked face.

Liddy focused on Gemma's bare feet. "What kind of shoes are you going to wear?"

"I have some white sandals I can strap on. Mom already spent enough on the dress," Gemma said.

"We're going shoe shopping when you get off school tomorrow. Consider it your graduation present. I will not have you wearing some ordinary sandals with that dress," Liddy said, slapping her hand on the counter to make her point. "There. It's settled."

"Wait. I totally forgot about getting you a graduation gift," Mona said.

"You don't need to get me anything, Aunt Mona," Gemma said. "Seriously."

"No, I do. I'm not going to let Liddy have all the glory. What do you want? Tell me. As long as it doesn't send my credit card over the limit. Again."

"Well, there is one thing . . ." Gemma said, giving her mother a playful wink.

"Just name it. You want a necklace? We can drive up to Zales and get a nice birthstone or something to go with the dress."

"Actually, what I really want is . . ." Gemma said, reaching out and taking Mona's hand. "Is for you to go to your high school reunion with Mom and Liddy."

Mona wrenched her hand free. "Did your nasty mother put you up to this?"

"You said *anything*," Gemma said. "And that's what I want."

"You people are pure evil," Mona said, gulping down the remainder of her wine.

"Then it's settled," Liddy said. "And don't worry, no matter what those overly made up clucking hens say or do, we will have a good time!"

Mona sat there scowling.

But Hayley sensed there might be a tiny part of her that might be looking forward to attending the reunion. She just had to keep up her dour exterior so as not to jeopardize her prickly reputation.

Hayley felt in her bones that it was going to be a memorable night.

She just had no idea how memorable.

Chapter 8

Hayley never imagined they could pull off a memorable reunion in such a short period of time, but from the moment her former classmates began pouring into the Kebo Valley Golf Club, hugging and laughing and snapping selfies to tweet out to family and friends, it quickly became clear the party was going to be a resounding success.

In the end, Sabrina, Nykki, and Ivy went with a minimum amount of decorations mostly because they got bored with the effort and were distracted by a private reunion dinner for their cheerleading squad and a few more boating outings with their rich friends.

That was fine by Hayley.

She was left in peace to make sure there was plenty of food for everyone without busting their budget.

Liddy and Mona showed up early to help set up

the tables of appetizers and after a quick count-
down of platters, everything was put out piping
hot and ready to serve.

The only item still heating up in the oven was
Hayley's tasty mini party quiches.

Hayley also enlisted the aid of her son, Dustin,
an aspiring filmmaker, to record the festivities on
his GoPro camera that he saved up for all last
summer from bagging groceries at the Shop 'n
Save. Dustin weaved in and out of all the clusters
of revelers grabbing priceless reactions of people
reunited with friends they hadn't seen in two
decades. Hayley had told Dustin not to get too
fancy, but the mini JJ Abrams was panning and
swishing as if this little video was destined to be a
finalist at the Cannes Film Festival.

As she removed tin foil off a crockpot of
Swedish meatballs that bubbled in a sea of gravy,
Hayley caught sight of Mona hugging a balding
man with a goatee, so small and fragile she feared
Mona might snap him in half. She didn't recognize him at first or the man with him, who was
almost as tiny and wearing a bright lime blazer
that matched his companion's. Then it dawned
on her.

Norman Langford.

Mona's prom date.

The dance captain from Rhode Island.

Mona, who had downed a few dirty martinis
before the cash bar even opened, was rosy-cheeked
and glassy-eyed and already having a marvelous
time. She and Norman were giggling and hugging

and then Mona hooked a meaty hand around the man next to Norman, presumably his husband, and pulled him into her bosom squeezing him so tight he fought for air.

Hayley knew in her gut if she could just get Mona to attend the reunion, she would ultimately have fun, and her feeling was right.

Hayley scanned the crowd.

Liddy was busy flirting with all her old boyfriends from high school.

Even the married ones.

Sabrina and Nykki were huddled with their clique of girls, most of whom were remarkably well preserved, a couple sporting bodies worthy of supermodels.

What the hell was their secret?

Hayley wondered where Ivy was with her self-proclaimed world famous cupcakes?

Maybe *that* was their secret to a slim figure.

Unlike Hayley, they weren't thinking about cupcakes.

Or food in general.

All the time.

Hayley was chomping at the bit to mingle with her former classmates. She noticed more arriving by the minute and it made her smile. All of these people from her past in one room. It was bringing back a lot of fond memories.

She was about to slip in line at the bar for a Jack and Coke and chat up Lisa O'Donnell, an old friend who sat in front of her in homeroom and who still lived in town and worked at the Harbor

Side Hotel, when she suddenly smelled something burning.

Her mini party quiches.

Hayley dashed into the kitchen and saw wisps of smoke billowing out of the oven. She grabbed an oven mitt off the counter and whipped open the door, waving the smoke away with her free hand.

The quiches were burnt to a crisp.

Hayley sighed as she took the pan out of the oven and dumped them into the large gray plastic garbage bin in the corner.

Still, after quickly calculating numbers in her mind, she figured they wouldn't be short of food before the night was over. If anything, Hayley usually made too much and there were always leftovers for weeks.

She was even contemplating writing a cook book one day.

Recipes using leftovers.

Now that would be a book she would buy.

She was rinsing the pan off in the sink when she suddenly felt something squeezing the flesh on her butt.

It was a hand.

A man's hand.

Hayley spun around to find herself face to face with Mason Cassidy.

Sabrina's impossibly handsome tattooed boy toy.

"What are you doing?"

"I've wanted to do that ever since I met you at

the bar the other day," Mason said, a wolfish grin on his face.

She slapped his hands away.

"Mason, stop it! Right now!"

"Older women like you drive me crazy," Mason said, moving in close to her, the scent of garlic on his breath making it obvious he had devoured a few of Hayley's Parmesan Garlic Chicken Wings before sneaking into the kitchen and copping a feel.

"You're with Sabrina! Get your hands off me!"

"She can't boil water. But you, you're a master in the kitchen, and I am a slave to any woman who can turn me on with her culinary talents."

Mason then pinned her against the counter, grabbing her wrists with his hands and covering Hayley's mouth with his own.

She struggled, but the muscled high diver was strong. He let go of one of her wrists to cup her neck with his hand as he thrust his tongue into her mouth even deeper.

Hayley used her free hand to reach up and slip a finger through the earring hole on his left ear lobe.

She yanked down hard.

Nearly tearing the flesh right off.

Mason yelped in pain and jerked his head back.

But he still had his arms around her, pinning her to the counter.

Suddenly there was a gasp from the doorway.

She cranked her head around to see Nykki, a hand over her mouth as she took in the scene.

Hayley knew if she said anything lame like "This is not what it looks like" it would just make matters worse.

So she just stood there with Mason hanging off her knowing how bad it looked.

Nykki's eyes blazed with anger as she turned on her white high heels that matched her skin tight cocktail dress and dashed out of the kitchen.

Hayley could feel her cheeks burning red and with all her might she slapped Mason hard across the face, wiping the twisted smile off his smug face.

"You ever touch me again, I will filet you like a fish. You hear me?"

Mason nodded.

The smile was back on his face.

Her rejection, her utter revulsion, just seemed to excite him even more.

Hayley pushed him away from her and raced out of the kitchen.

Chapter 9

Hayley flew out through the silver swinging doors leading into the main dining room and scanned the crowd, many of whom at this point were jiggling and gyrating on the makeshift dance floor to Janet Jackson.

She spotted Nykki, who had already found Sabrina.

They were standing near the bar.

Nykki's hands gesticulated wildly as she presumably recounted the horror of what she had just witnessed in the kitchen.

Sabrina listened to her intently, a crestfallen look on her face.

Hayley knew she had to explain what happened with Mason.

She began to weave through the crowd, ducking her head at one point to avoid getting struck by a woman she didn't recognize in a cream colored gown shaking and shimmying as if she was having some kind of seizure. Probably a spouse she hadn't met yet.

Before she could make it all the way across the dance floor, a man stepped in front of her, blocking her route.

"Hayley Powell! You haven't changed a bit! Do you remember me?" the man asked, his high pitched voice cracking as if he were still struggling through puberty after all these years.

He was heavy set with a healthy gut.

His drab brown sports jacket seemed three sizes too small for him and the buttons on his shirt strained against his girth, threatening to pop off.

"Charles? It's so nice to see you. You haven't changed much either," Hayley lied, peering over his shoulder to make sure Sabrina didn't run out of the reunion in tears before she had a chance to relate her side of the story.

Charles McNally was the former student council president in high school.

Back then, he was quite a catch.

State champion cross-country runner.

Politically active successfully battling the school administration for a soda machine to be installed in the cafeteria.

A weekend volunteer with Habitat for Humanity going around the state building homes for the needy.

And with wavy blond hair, most of which was gone now, and fresh-faced good looks, he was the topic of many discussions in the back row of study hall between Sabrina and her posse, all of whom had massive crushes on him and were determined to find themselves on his radar.

In the end, it was Ivy who emerged the lucky victor after winning the vice president spot on the student council, though Hayley and her pals were convinced there was some underhanded ballot box stuffing to insure she won. Working on a number of projects after school and well into the night, it was only a matter of time before their hormones got the best of them and they began dating.

They lasted through all of senior year. She dumped him during the summer after graduation. Charles was devasted and never really recovered. It even affected his studies at Wesleyan that fall.

Charles got a scholarship to Wesleyan in Connecticut and Ivy went off to Sarah Lawrence in New York because her mother was a treasured alumnus. He let the pressures of continuing to be the best at everything get the better of him and he found himself smack dab in the middle of a cheating scandal after hiring a brainy kid to take his final exams for him. He was instantly expelled and life for Charles went downhill fast. He never recovered. Once a shining star, he was now an academic washout and Hayley heard a rumor he was pumping gas at a Chevron station just outside of Hartford through most of his twenties. Which was good honest work, but not what the ambitious Charles McNally had in mind for himself. After that, she lost track of him until he joined the Mount Desert Island High School reunion group on Facebook and posted he was planning to attend.

"What have you been up to?" Hayley asked, her eyes still locked on Sabrina, who was now downing a drink she had just grabbed off the bar as Nykki continued to talk her ear off.

"Well, not many people know this but I created an app called Designated Driver where people at bars can sign up and with one click a driver will find you through your phone's GPS and get you home safely. I've done very well with it. *Very* well," he said, making sure his point was made.

"Like Uber, but for heavy drinkers," Hayley said.

"Something like that. I'm in a much better place than I was ten years ago, which was why I skipped our first reunion. How have you been, Hayley?"

"Well, I have two kids, Gemma and Dustin—"

"Is Ivy here?"

So much for his interest in her life since high school.

"I haven't seen her. But she will be here. She's bringing cupcakes."

"I read about her successful business. Very impressive. I always knew Ivy would be a major player in the world of business."

Major player?

Okay, her cupcakes were tasty.

But she wasn't exactly running General Motors.

"Listen, I was wondering," Charles said, leaning in to Hayley to shout in her ear above the music, which was now cranked up even louder as everybody rocked out to the dance remix of Annie Lennox's "No More I Love You's". "Is Ivy—?"

Hayley knew the question before he even asked it. "Yes, Charles. I'm afraid Ivy's married. Her husband is here in town with her."

Charles looked as if the wind had just been knocked out of him.

His whole body sagged and his sad eyes resembled those of a puppy just swatted on the behind with a newspaper after peeing on the floor.

"I'm sorry, Charles. I can tell you still harbor feelings for her."

"I guess it was foolish of me to expect a woman like Ivy to be single and available. Of course she has to be happily married."

"Well, to be honest, happily might be too strong a word," Hayley said as she watched Ivy blow through the door carrying a large pink box with her husband Nigel running behind her.

"There she is," Hayley said.

Charles' eyes widened. "*That's* her husband?"

"Yes. Why? Do you know him?"

Charles didn't bother answering her.

His gaze had already floated over to Ivy. "She looks absolutely beautiful."

"Please don't cause a scene!" Nigel screamed at his wife, although his voice was nearly drowned out by the thumping music.

Nigel reached out to stop Ivy by grabbing her arm.

She tried to shake free but his grip tightened.

"Can we just go back outside and talk about this?" Nigel yelled.

"No!" Ivy screamed, wrenching her arm free before spinning around to escape from him and tripping over her high heeled shoes. She managed to regain her balance but the pink box flew out of her arms and landed with a thud on the floor while four cupcakes with sprinkles were ejected and splattered on the dance floor, some cream filling even landing on the tip of Charles' polished shoe.

"Now look at what you made me do!" Ivy wailed above the music. The festive mood was instantly broken as people stopped dancing to gawk at the embarrassing scene. The DJ, drawn to the commotion, even lowered the volume so he could hear what the feuding couple was saying.

"Relax. There are four more boxes in the car. Plenty to go around," Nigel said in his clipped English voice, his face red with humiliation as everyone watched this sad depiction of a crumbling marriage like out of an Edward Albee play. "I'll go get them."

"Don't touch them! I just want you to leave! Go back to the house. Hell, go back to England for all I care! Just leave me in peace so I can spend time with my friends and be happy for the first time in years!" she screamed.

Ivy fled into the kitchen passing Mason, who was standing near the swinging doors having just come out himself.

He wasn't paying much attention to the drama unfolding in front of him.

He was more interested in staring across the room at Sabrina, who had regained her composure and was now focused on her good friend Ivy's ill-timed meltdown.

The whole room just stood there watching Nigel, curious to know what he would do next.

It was a supremely uncomfortable moment for everyone.

Except for Charles McNally.

He beamed with utter delight.

Because as of this moment, the odds of Ivy Foster ending up back on the market had just increased significantly.

Chapter 10

Nigel looked around the room, realizing all eyes were upon him.

He quickly collected himself and then turned and marched out the door.

Hayley noticed her son Dustin recording the entire ugly scene on his camera, thrilled to be documenting such high drama, and giving his mother an enthusiastic thumbs up.

She suddenly felt a hand rest gently on her shoulder.

"Hayley, do you think I should go into the kitchen and talk to Ivy? I think she could really use a shoulder to cry on," Charles McNally said, forgetting to wipe the delirious smile off his face.

"No, Charles. I really don't think that would be such a good idea right now," Hayley said.

"You're right. I should have a couple of cocktails first, you know, fill up on some liquid courage, just to take the edge off before I go for it."

Charles ambled over to the bar, raising a pudgy

index finger to attract the attention of the bartender.

The door to the golf club flew open again before the DJ had a chance to crank the volume of the music back up, and the crowd was jarred by a cacophony of familiar ear-splitting high pitched yelping.

Ivy's seven toy poodles.

Nigel, face full of rage, stormed through the crowd, dragging the dogs by their leashes, the leather straps all tethered together in Nigel's hammy white knuckled fists. One of the dogs, maybe Sleepy but who really knows, was too slow and couldn't keep up. Nigel didn't slow down; he just yanked the leashes harder, and the poor little guy lost his balance and wound up being dragged across the hardwood floor on his butt.

With his free hand, Nigel slammed open the swinging doors, the dogs still yelping and yapping behind him, and disappeared into the kitchen where the crowd heard more loud shouting.

"If you truly want me to leave, I am not going to be stuck with these glorified rats! Take them! Let's see how well you can handle them without me around to buy them treats and pick them up from the groomers!" Nigel cried.

"Good riddance!" they heard Ivy scream. "They never liked you anyway!"

Hayley signaled the DJ who finally turned up the music, drowning out the warring couple in the kitchen.

But people were no longer in the mood to dance.

Most were gathered around in little groups to gossip about what they had just witnessed.

A few minutes passed before Nigel stomped out of the kitchen, this time without the dogs in tow, passing Sabrina and Nykki, who were in a corner by themselves still engaged in an intense discussion.

They never even bothered to look up when Nigel blew past them and out the door this time for good.

Unlike the rest of their classmates, Sabrina and Nykki couldn't be less interested in the public meltdown of their best friend Ivy's marriage.

It appeared they had something far more serious to talk about.

But if Nykki was detailing what she had witnessed between Hayley and Mason in the kitchen earlier, why was it taking Sabrina so long to march over to Hayley and confront her about it?

Mona stumbled over to Hayley, a dopey grin on her face, swishing around the remnants of her sixth or seventh cocktail in the bottom of her plastic cup. "I got to hand it to you, Hayley. I'm glad you and Gemma forced me to come. This is the best reunion ever!"

"See? I knew you'd enjoy reconnecting with old friends if you just gave it a chance, Mona," Hayley said.

"Hell, no. That's not what I'm talking about. I mean, watching that nasty mean girl Ivy cause such an embarrassing scene and make a complete ass of herself, well, I couldn't have dreamed of a better time!"

Mona slurped down the rest of her drink and wandered away toward the bar.

Hayley turned her attention back to Sabrina and Nykki.

They were no longer huddled together in deep discussion.

They were now staring over at the table where Liddy sat to greet the late stragglers and collect the twenty dollar entrance fee and hand them their name tag. There were just three or four tags left to be claimed but none of them belonged to the robust, full figured woman in a ratty gray sweater full of holes, a housedress in dire need of a wash, and a red weathered Boston Celtics cap with scuff marks, the visor fraying at the edges.

She looked like a homeless person.

And for all Hayley knew, she was.

It was Vanda Spears.

Vanda was in Hayley's class through most of middle school and part of high school. She was an eccentric girl to say the least—some might say crazy—who had a habit of talking to herself and disappearing into her own little world. She was constantly being sent to the school psychiatrist for evaluation, but her parents refused to accept the fact that there was anything wrong with her. They simply chalked it up to her being creative and a free spirit.

But it was clear Vanda was unlike the other kids in her class. And when someone is different, they frequently become the target of bullies. Vanda was certainly no exception. When she was younger, boys would push her down into mud puddles on the playground or grab her from behind and force her face into a snow bank during the winter. They would call her names and kick the back of her seat on the school bus.

And the girls in Vanda's class were even worse. Particularly when Vanda entered high school and the cliques began to grow into little armies of pettiness and aggression. The most vicious bunch of all of course was Sabrina, Nykki, and Ivy, who took a perverse pleasure in humiliating her in front of everyone. They convinced her that the captain of the basketball team had a huge crush on her and forged a Valentine's Day card from him professing his love. When Vanda tried to kiss him in the cafeteria he pushed her away so violently she fell into a table and knocked it over, trays of mystery meat and lumpy mashed potatoes sliding off and covering her head. She dropped out of school shortly during sophomore year never to return.

Hayley had seen her around town from time to time.

She had heard Vanda had been in and out of various mental health facilities. Her parents had long since passed away and were no longer around to help her get by. Rumor had it she had a sympathetic cousin in Florida who would put her up in St. Petersburg during the winter, but Vanda missed the island and would pop up during the spring and summer months to walk the streets. God only knew where she stayed while in town. Maybe under a tree in Acadia National Park, avoiding the rangers who might catch her after closing hours.

Liddy moved aside and allowed Vanda to jaunt merrily through the crowd smiling and nodding to her former classmates.

Hayley rushed over to her.

"What's Vanda Spears doing here?"

"I have no idea," Liddy gasped. "But she was insistent that I let her in so she could spend time with some of her old friends."

A few people smiled nervously at Vanda as she stopped to say hello, whereas others turned their backs, pretending not to see her.

"I guess there's no harm in letting her stay even though she didn't pay like everybody else," Hayley said.

Hayley suddenly felt her arm yank back and she was spun around by Nykki, who was standing shoulder to shoulder with Sabrina, both with mortified looks on their faces.

"Hayley, how could you let Vanda Spears in here?" Nykki asked in an urgent hushed voice. "You know she wasn't in our class!"

"Technically she was. She just didn't graduate with us," Hayley said.

"That's no excuse. You need to ask her to leave right now," Sabrina whispered, clutching her chest with one hand as if she were having heart palpitations.

"I really don't see the harm in letting her stay," Hayley said.

"She's a bonafide looney tune and she's going to ruin the reunion for everybody unless you get her out now!" Nykki wailed.

"I don't understand. Why do you care so much?" Liddy asked, taking a perverse pleasure in watching her nemesis Nykki suddenly becoming so unhinged.

"Please, just do it!" Sabrina begged.

There was an eruption of barking in the kitchen.

The dogs were at it again.

Out of the corner of her eye, Hayley saw Charles McNally button a button on his shirt that had popped open revealing his belly button, and then steeling himself as he walked into the kitchen, finally emboldened enough, or drunk enough, to seize his opportunity to comfort his beloved Ivy.

"Where is she? I don't see her," Liddy said.

"Who?" Hayley asked, drawn back into the conversation.

"Vanda. Do you think she left?"

"Let's hope so," Nykki said with a sigh.

Suddenly rising above the din of the dogs barking was a man's anguished cry.

It was coming from the kitchen.

The swinging doors burst open and Charles McNally, his arms raised in the air, his face a frozen mask of grief and horror, stumbled out.

He could barely speak.

He just pointed toward the kitchen.

Leading the charge, Hayley dashed across the room with Liddy, Nykki, and Sabrina close on her heels. They were followed by a swarm of other startled and curious classmates. They all poured into the kitchen and stopped short at the grisly sight of Ivy Foster lying face down on the floor surrounded by her signature butter cream cupcakes as her devoted pack of tiny toy poodles named after the seven dwarves danced around her body yipping and yapping and howling in a panicked frenzy.

Island Food & Spirits
by
Hayley Powell

It is peak tourist season and that can only mean one thing. The police scanner on top of my refrigerator is buzzing a lot more with news of out-of-towner drama. In the last hour alone, there was one fender bender at the head of the island, one lost child on a mountain trail, a carry out off Dorr Mountain (which is usually someone who left the trail, slipped, and broke a leg or arm), a domestic disturbance at one of the hotels (too much vacation celebration with alcohol), and, last but not least, a car about to be submerged underwater at Bar Island.

This last one happens all the time in the summer because Bar Island is a big attraction for the tourists that visit Bar Harbor. One can access the island from West Street at the waterfront. A short road takes you right to the little rocky beach that overlooks the ocean. To your right is the town pier and the vast ocean, and to your left are the lovely old waterfront mansions and more ocean. But when low tide comes, water recedes and almost like magic a natural gravel land bridge opens up (the locals call it the bar) and you can walk or even drive your car over to the island to have a picnic, hike, or just explore. It's a fun way to spend some time on an island for a few hours.

Unfortunately, some people do not realize that you only have a certain amount of time between low and high tide, and for those who have not checked their tide charts, or have failed to do a little research on the subject, they will arrive to explore it and see the path across wide open, not realizing the tide is coming in and they will pretty soon find themselves in a very sticky situation.

God knows I've seen this happen with tourists time and time again.

Last summer after indulging with a couple of delicious Cape Codder cocktails, I decided to take Leroy for a short walk. We headed to Bar Island so Leroy could chase seagulls and sniff shells. The tide wouldn't be fully high for a couple of hours.

During the summer there were always a few locals like me there with their dogs or kids running around taking advantage of a beautiful post-dinner evening. It was fun to gossip and catch up with people you didn't have the chance to see all the time. When the tide came in and started to cover the path between the mainland and the island, we called the dogs and kids back to head home, since it would begin a fast rise now.

That's when we noticed that no one had yet come for the car that was parked almost right in the middle of the bar. This happens more often than not with the many tourists who visit here, but we noticed that this particular car had a Maine license plate, which was surprising since we locals pride ourselves on our expert knowledge about tides.

"Could be a rental," I snorted. "Can't be a local."

It was a newer looking Mazda-type car. The sunroof was wide open and the water was just now beginning to creep up the sides of the tires.

No one was really worried yet because this unfortunately was a pretty normal occurrence. As the minutes passed and the tide rose higher and higher, now almost completely above the car's tires, I decided it might be a good idea to give Chief Alvarez of the Bar Harbor Police Department a heads up with a quick phone call in case the owner did not return so he could at least send a tow truck for the car as the water was now up above the sides of the doors.

I punched the number into my cell phone and asked for the chief and was told by the night dispatcher Debbie that he was on another line, but since she knew the chief and I were family by marriage, she informed me he was talking to a worried local mother who was upset because her newly licensed teenage son had not yet returned home after borrowing her brand new Mazda over four hours ago.

I gasped and told her to interrupt the chief because I believed that there might be a possibility that this was the same car out on the bar and they had better hurry because the car was going to be completely underwater soon.

As I hung up and glanced at the rising tide that was now up to the car's windows, I relayed the information I learned to the growing crowd on the beach.

Just then a truck came roaring down the street and screeched to a stop as a woman jumped out of the passenger side and came running toward us screaming that the car was hers and where was her son?

I immediately recognized her. Sarah Cumberland (I've changed her name to protect the not-so-innocent). We were on the same sports boosters committee and our kids went to high school together. She was always trying to outdo me when it was our turn to provide snacks for the school sporting events. She would show up with her "famous" (or so she said) Cranberry Cream Cheese Bars and make a big fuss about placing them front and center on the table. That was usually followed by a snide remark about the brownies or cookies I had brought. But at least I followed the food list that had been emailed to me instead of "going rogue" like she always did.

We could now hear the police and fire trucks' sirens getting closer.

This was turning into quite the drama so (and I must say with a little delight) I called my boss at the paper so he could get a photographer there and take a few pictures for tomorrow's edition with his telephoto lens. There was no sense in wasting a good photo opportunity.

Now there was nothing left to do but wait, hoping the woman's son would be spotted on the beach waving for help.

Just then, two police cars and a fire truck arrived but still no tow truck because we were told they were busy dealing with a fender bender in Town Hill and by the time the one from Southwest Harbor could get there it would be too late to save the car, which by now was almost totally submerged.

I couldn't resist commenting to a few of my fellow gawkers that this woman needed to keep a better eye on her kid especially nowadays when every teenager has a cell phone. It's so easy to check in to prevent something like this from happening. I know it's petty, but I took a perverse joy in the woman's predicament, mostly because she was always showing me up in front of the other parents.

Just then, two small figures emerged from the woods and ran to the water's edge screaming and waving their arms and jumping up and down yelling for help.

Chief Alvarez grabbed a bull horn from his police cruiser and told the frightened teens that a boat was on the way and if they could hear him to stop jumping and just wave. They followed his instructions.

We all sighed with relief when just a few minutes later we saw a park ranger boat come into view. They loaded up the huddled teens and ferried them back to the mainland.

Sarah looked so relieved to see her son safe and sound even as she yelled at him from across the bay that he wouldn't be driving a car for a long time! It reminded me to check in on my own daughter. I called her cell and when she answered she seemed distracted. She started to explain but then the crowd erupted in cheers as the park ranger delivered the teens safely to shore, drowning out her voice. As the rangers helped the teenage boy out of the boat, right behind him I spotted a teenage girl, holding a cell phone to her ear. I did a double take! It was my daughter being escorted off the boat by a helpful park ranger. Out of the corner of my eye I noticed a few people nodding and nudging each other while pointing at me. I knew I deserved it. I tightened my grip on Leroy's leash and marched over to the boat and my embarrassed daughter.

Lesson learned.

There was going to be another teen who wouldn't be driving for a long time!

Cape Codder

<u>Ingredients:</u>

3 ounces cranberry juice
2 ounces vodka
lime wedge to garnish

Fill a glass with ice and the first two ingredients and garnish with a lime wedge.

This is a delicious cocktail that every New Englander indulges in at one time or another!

All that talk about Cranberry Cream Cheese Bars got me thinking. I had my own recipe stuffed away somewhere. Sarah Cumberland is not the only one who can make them. My mother swears it was her great great grandmother's recipe but unless her great great grandmother was Betty Crocker I have my doubts. But no matter where she got it, these tasty, sweet Cranberry Cream Cheese Bars are a hit at any party.

Cranberry Cream Cheese Bars

Ingredients:

1 stick room temperature butter
1½ cups sugar
2 eggs
1½ cups flour
½ teaspoon salt
1 teaspoon baking powder
2 cups fresh whole cranberries
½ cup chopped pecans

Preheat your oven to 350 degrees, and grease a 13x9 inch baking pan.

In a large bowl cream together the butter and sugar, beat in the eggs and vanilla.

Then add your flour, salt, baking powder, cranberries, and pecans.

Spread the batter in the greased baking pan.

Bake in the oven for 35 to 40 minutes until a toothpick comes out clean.

Remove from oven and cool completely.

Frosting

Ingredients:

2½ cups confectionary sugar
4 ounce block of cream cheese room
    temperature

¼ cup butter room temperature
1 tablespoon milk
1 teaspoon vanilla

Mix all of the ingredients together and spread over the cooled bars. When ready, cut into squares and serve.

Chapter 11

Hayley had no idea who called 911, but within five minutes Police Chief Sergio Alvares and two of his officers, Donnie and Earl, were bursting through the doors of the Kebo Valley Golf Club. Sergio ordered his men to clear the kitchen of gawkers, corral all of the party guests, and detain them in the main dining room while he inspected the dead body in the kitchen.

After a few minutes, Sergio returned and asked the crowd who had discovered the body.

Charles McNally tentatively raised his hand and then was quickly escorted to a side office to be questioned by Sergio.

Ivy's seven dogs were still barking and yelping and skittering all over the place so Officer Earl chased them down one by one, gathering up their leashes and hauling them outside where he locked them in the backseat of a squad car so they would not be in the way.

Hayley scanned the nervous crowd as they murmured and shook their heads, not quite believing what was happening. No one was quite ready to grasp the fact that a death had occurred right in the middle of their high school reunion.

The sight of Ivy's prone body had sobered up Mona and she wasn't happy about it. Hayley knew when Mona had a pounding headache because she stopped bellowing. Mostly because the sound of her own booming voice exacerbated the pain. Mona retreated to a corner where she sat quietly licking the frosting off a butter cream cupcake. Hayley could only hope that she hadn't picked it up off the floor in the kitchen during the commotion.

There was a loud scuffle by the front door that suddenly drew everyone's attention. Officer Earl struggled with two women who were apparently trying to slip out while no one was noticing, but he spotted them when he was coming back from herding the poodles into his squad car.

It was Sabrina and Nykki.

Sabrina clawed at Earl's fingers which were tightly circled around her upper forearm. "Let go of me!"

"I'm sorry, ma'am, nobody goes anywhere until the chief has had a chance to talk to everyone," Earl said, his cheeks reddening as Sabrina's nails dug into his skin.

Nykki also fought hard against the young officer's grip but she was more resigned to the fact that a quick escape was unlikely.

Why would Sabrina and Nykki be so anxious to flee the scene?

Didn't they care to find out what happened to their best friend?

It didn't make any sense.

Once they realized all eyes in the room were staring at them, both women calmed down, shook free of Officer Earl, and raced to a corner together to huddle and whisper to each other.

Hayley was about to walk over and ask them point blank what was going on when Officer Donnie sauntered into the room followed by a devastated Charles McNally, his face a ghostly white, his shoulders hunched over in grief. He plopped down in a chair and covered his puffy face with his hands and silently cried.

"Hayley Powell, the chief would like to speak to you next," Officer Donnie announced, waving her over.

Hayley followed Officer Donnie into the side office where Sergio waited.

Before Sergio had a chance to speak, Hayley asked, "Do you know what happened to her?"

"It looks like a blow to the back of the head killed her instantly. She dropped to the floor like a sack of pears."

Potatoes.

Sack of potatoes.

Hayley had long given up on correcting native Brazilian Sergio's sometimes spotty grasp of English phrases.

"So someone murdered her?" Hayley said, stunned.

"I am not going to announce anything until the new coroner has conducted a complete autopsy," Sergio said. "But I saw the head wound and it looked pretty bad."

The only reason Hayley was given access to this new information was because Sergio was aware of the fact that Hayley had a knack for solving crimes and she would probably find out on her own eventually anyway so why not just cut to the chase?

"Mr. McNally told me the victim had a fight with her husband a few minutes before the body was discovered?"

"That's right," Hayley said. "Nigel. But he left before it happened."

"He could have doubled back. There was another entrance to the kitchen near the eighteenth hole. I've already radioed my officers to find him and bring him in. Know where they can find him?"

"I would start with the rental house where they were staying in Seal Harbor. Sabrina and her . . . friend are staying there too. She can give you the address."

"Is there anyone else you can think of who has a bulge for Ivy?"

"I beg your pardon?"

"You know what I'm talking about. A bulge."

"You mean besides Charles McNally?"

"Mr. McNally had a bulge?"

"When it came to Ivy, absolutely."

"I'm surprised. He seemed so broken up over her death."

"Exactly. Because he had the hots for her."

"The what?"

This conversation was going off the rails.

Hayley took a deep breath. She remembered she was communicating with her English-challenged brother-in-law and then reviewed their discussion.

That's when it hit her.

"You mean grudge! A *grudge* against the victim!"

"Bulge. Grudge. Don't they mean the the same thing?"

"Not even close."

Sergio sighed, frustrated. "English is not my first language, okay? So cut me some grass."

"Cut me some slack," Hayley said under her breath but loud enough for Sergio to hear.

"Slack? What is slack? How do you *cut* slack? Why do you Americans have to always make everything so complicated?"

"Let's try to get back on track here."

"Track? Is that anything like slack?"

"Sergio! You asked me if anybody else had a grudge against . . . didn't *like* Ivy, and honestly the only person I can think of is *me*!"

That stopped Sergio . . . in his tracks. "*You?*"

Hayley went on to briefly explain her painful history with Ivy as well as Sabrina and Nykki but for some inexplicable reason she failed to bring him up to speed on Sabrina and Nykki's suspicious attempt to slip away from the crime scene just moments before. She was sure Earl would fill the chief in on all the details himself, and Hayley didn't want to come off as a snitch.

Sergio nodded and took notes.

"Okay, Hayley. That's it for now. You're free to go. I may have some more questions for you later but I know where to find you," he said, smiling. "Donnie!"

Officer Donnie poked his head in. "Yes, Chief?"

"Bring in Mona Barnes."

"Mona . . ." Donnie's voice trailed off. He looked like a child too young for Disneyland, who reacts with fear at the sight of a giant Goofy approaching.

"You heard me," Sergio said, a little more forcefully.

"Chief, you promised me I would never have to deal with *that* woman ever again!" Donnie wailed.

Mona and Officer Donnie had come to blows once when Mona was considered a suspect in another murder investigation.

And frankly she whipped his butt.

Ever since then the poor kid was a bundle of nerves whenever he was in the same vicinity fearing she might lash out unexpectedly like an alligator stepped on by an unsuspecting hiker splashing through a swamp.

"Never mind. I will go get her myself," Sergio said, standing up and blowing past his young officer. Hayley tried not to giggle but Donnie was so spooked by the prospect of having to talk to his sworn enemy.

At least in his mind.

Mona could barely remember his name.

When Hayley stepped back into the main room, she spied Sabrina and Nykki eyeing the door as if plotting yet another escape.

They were downright panicked at the idea of being questioned by the police.

And it aroused Hayley's already insatiable curiosity.

Suddenly a hand touched the small of her back.

Hayley spun around to see Aaron standing there.

He was in blue jeans and a tight-fitting gray t-shirt that accentuated his muscles.

His hotness made her feel all warm inside.

"I heard what was happening on the scanner at your house so I decided to come and make sure you were okay," he said, hugging her.

Hayley didn't want to let go.

She said in his ear, "I'm so glad you're here."

"What can I do?"

Hayley finally pulled away from him. "You can drive me home. I came with Mona and she still has to be questioned by Sergio, and I just want to get the hell out of here before I burst into tears in front of everyone."

Aaron took her hand. "Then let's go."

He led her out the door past Officer Earl, who was guarding the exit.

He nodded as they passed him.

Hayley glanced back at Sabrina and Nykki, who watched her enviously as she left them behind.

When they got into Aaron's car and closed the doors, Hayley lost it.

Her face was a flood of tears.

Aaron stopped buckling himself in and reached over and gently guided her head to his chest.

As Hayley let it all out, Aaron brushed her hair softly with the palm of his hand.

He was so strong.

"It's going to be okay," Aaron said, almost in a whisper.

"I'm going to find out who did this," Hayley choked out during sobs, surprised at herself for having such an emotional reaction to Ivy Foster's death.

Someone who was barely ever nice to her.

But a death is a death.

And no one, not even catty cupcake queen Ivy Foster, deserved to die so violently and viciously.

Aaron didn't respond to Hayley.

He didn't have to.

Because Aaron had been around long enough now to know Hayley's history.

And her single-minded determination to get to the truth.

When they had started dating, he thought he was dating a simple single mother of two who wrote a cute food and cocktails column.

Only later did he discover that he was dating a true crime investigative journalist who also just happened to be a kick-ass cook.

Chapter 12

When Hayley and Aaron pulled into the driveway of her house, Hayley was surprised to notice all the lights turned off inside.

She knew Dustin was over at his buddy Spanky's because they were partners in the upcoming science fair and were testing their potato-powered clock.

But Gemma should have been home by now.

They got out of the car and entered the kitchen through the back door off the side deck. Aaron squeezed Hayley's hand protectively, letting her know that he was right there with her.

Hayley stopped and listened.

She heard sniffling.

It was coming from the living room.

Leroy scampered into the kitchen, tail wagging, running around in circles and then dashing back into the hallway, trying to signal Hayley to follow him. He was just like Lassie at the end of the movie leading the adults to where Timmy had fallen into the well.

Hayley let go of Aaron's hand and motioned for him to stay in the kitchen while she investigated. She was very familiar with that sniffling sound. It sounded just like Gemma when she was upset.

Sure enough, as Hayley rounded the corner into the living room she was able to make out her teenage daughter curled up in a ball on the couch, her face buried in her knees, illuminated just enough by the moonlight streaming through the window.

"Honey, what's wrong?" Hayley said sitting down next to her and placing a hand on her shoulder.

Gemma kept her face firmly planted against her knees and shook her head. "I don't want to talk about it."

"Well, you're going to have to sometime so why not just do it now and get it over with? Who knows? Maybe I can help."

This last statement was shocking enough to get Gemma to pop her head up and raise her eyebrow skeptically.

The idea of her mother being remotely capable of actually helping her through a crisis was too much for Gemma to ignore.

Hayley noticed Blueberry hiding his massive bulk underneath the TV stand, hyperaware of the emotional tension and trying to avoid it at all costs. Unlike Leroy, this oversize fur ball with an attitude could definitely *not* be counted on in a crisis.

Gemma's eyes fell on Leroy who sat on his

haunches staring up at her from the floor, a concerned look in his eye.

"Stop staring at me, Leroy!" Gemma said loud enough for the little dog to take the hint. He scampered back into the kitchen to keep Aaron company.

Hayley could hear Aaron filling the coffee maker with freshly ground beans. He was obviously trying to stay busy and keep a respectful distance in order to give mother and daughter some privacy.

"Can you at least give me an idea of what's upset you so much?" Hayley said, stroking her daughter's back.

Gemma reached between the couch cushions and yanked out her cell phone. She tapped in her security code and then thrust the screen in her mother's face. "See for yourself!"

Hayley didn't have her reading glasses on so it took some squinting and holding the phone really close before she could make out the text.

Sorry. Can't make prom. Hope you didn't already buy the dress.

The text had been sent just under an hour ago.

"Oh no," Hayley said, her heart sinking. "Do you know why he had to cancel?"

Gemma angrily wiped the tears off her face with the arm of her light green sweatshirt. "I texted him right back to find out but he never bothered to answer me."

"Well, maybe it's some kind of family emergency."

"It's *not* a family emergency, Mom," Gemma scoffed. "Twenty minutes ago I got a call from my friend Stacy who saw Nate sucking face with Tina Leighton at Pat's Pizza in Ellsworth!"

"Who's Tina Leighton?"

"A total slut!"

"Gemma!"

"Sorry. I didn't mean slut. Tina Leighton's a mean-spirited nasty *whore*!"

"Gemma! You know I won't tolerate you calling another girl names like that."

"I know! But shouldn't it be okay if it's *true*?"

"No!"

"Fine. Sorry. Tina goes to Ellsworth High School and last September she met Nate when our football team played an away game against their team. Nate had a knee injury so he couldn't play so he spent the whole game on the bench flirting with Ellsworth's pom pom girls, especially Tina, and they were an item by Homecoming. But during Christmas vacation, Tina met a college boy home from Dartmouth, and dumped Nate. He was heartbroken. We all felt so sorry for him and we hated Tina for hurting him so bad. Nate was inconsolable. But slowly he healed and by spring he was back to his old self and that's why I was so thrilled when he asked me to be his date for the prom."

"So I'm guessing the college boy dumped Tina recently?"

"Yes. For his Ethics professor!"

"Wait. His *Ethics* professor is dating one of her college students? There are so many things wrong with that scenario!"

"Mother, please do not get side-tracked. This is *my* life we're talking about."

"Right. Sorry. Go on."

"Well, Tina wasted no time getting her hooks back into Nate because she's one of those girls who just can't stay single for long. And now *I'm* paying the price!"

"If Nate was so willing to jump right back in with Tina, then maybe he's not the kind of guy you should be dating."

Hayley couldn't resist lecturing her daughter on the uselessness of pining for an unworthy boy.

And she paid for it by having to endure one of her daughter's classic deadpan angry glares.

These were not the motherly words of wisdom Gemma expected or wanted.

Hayley couldn't let it go.

She didn't want her daughter's self-esteem to suffer at the hands of an undeserving cad.

"I mean, honestly, I think you're better off."

She really had to just stop talking.

At this point, Gemma looked like she was going to explode.

"That doesn't really help me with a prom date, now does it? All my friends are going to have a night to remember and I'm going to be stuck at home with you watching old episodes of *American Horror Story* on Netflix!" Gemma snorted before bounding off the couch and running up the stairs to her bedroom.

She punctuated her frustration by slamming her door shut.

Hayley had no intention of following her.

The best course of action was to leave her in peace for now.

And try to figure out a solution later.

Aaron slowly entered the living room holding two piping hot steaming fresh cups of coffee.

Hayley gratefully took one and blew on it before taking a long sip.

Aaron sat down next to her and put an arm around her, drawing her closer.

"God, I hate proms," she said.

"I had a blast at mine," Aaron said without thinking before catching himself. "I mean, as far as proms go."

"Well, mine was a disaster. It was like Carrie's. But without the pig's blood."

There was no response from Aaron.

He was probably still trying to shake the image of Sissy Spacek standing under a mirror ball, drenched in blood, eyes blazing, about to tele-kinetically take down her entire graduating class.

Hayley now had two missions.

Find a way to prevent her daughter from having to live with a terrible memory of her senior prom like her mother.

And find the person responsible for whacking her former frenemy in the back of the head and killing her.

Chapter 13

Hayley rang the bell twice at the seaside cottage in Seal Harbor that Nykki had rented for herself, Sabrina, Ivy, and their significant others while they were in town for the reunion.

There was no answer.

She noticed Nykki's rental car parked in the gravel driveway.

Were they inside and just not answering?

She was about to turn around and walk back to her car, but her suspicious nature got the best of her. She circled around to the back of the house that was nestled in a wooded area just two hundred feet from the rocky shore.

Just as she suspected, Nykki and Sabrina were sprawled out on a pair of matching striped chaise lounges on the deck that jutted out from the back of the house.

Nykki was pouring what looked like lemonade from a crystal decanter into a tall glass and handed it to Sabrina, who grabbed it with a shaky hand and downed it in one long gulp.

Hayley was fairly certain the thirst-quenching lemonade was spiked with something much stronger.

Sabrina was in a one-piece pink bathing suit that was mostly covered by a flower print wrap that blew in the wind. Nykki wore white Capri pants and a light green and blue striped top, obviously going for the Jackie Kennedy in Hyannis Port look. Both women looked drawn and pale as if neither had much sleep, which was understandable given the violent circumstances surrounding Ivy's death.

But Hayley knew there was more to the story, and was determined to find out what the women were so upset about.

Instead of making her presence immediately known, Hayley ducked down on her hands and knees and slowly made her way toward them from behind the hedges that lined the side of the house. Her hands and kneecaps were covered in dirt by the time she reached the edge of the porch.

Hayley strained to hear what the two women were saying to each other, but the waves rolling in with the tide crashed against the rocks on the shore, completely drowning them out.

She knew she had to get closer.

She waited until Nykki picked up the decanter and poured Sabrina another serving of the lemonade cocktail.

Nykki turned enough so her back was to Hayley.

Sabrina's eyes were hidden behind a giant pair of Calvin Klein sunglasses. She was staring out at the ocean and did not even notice Hayley climb up onto the porch and scurry over behind a potted plant, wedging herself between the large leafy flowers and the sliding glass door that led inside the house. She was now only a few feet from Sabrina and Nykki and could finally hear most of their conversation.

"What if she talks? Then what?" Sabrina wailed. "Who will believe her?"

"I can't go to prison, Nykki. I binge watched *Orange is the New Black* last winter and it made me sick. I could never live like that."

"Sabrina, you need to calm down. No one is going to prison. You just need to keep your cool. Let me handle this."

Handle what?

And who were they talking about?

Who had some serious dirt on the two of them?

Suddenly they were interrupted by a dog barking inside the house.

They both perked up and turned their heads toward Hayley's hiding place.

She crouched down even further hoping they wouldn't spot her.

That's when she noticed that on the other side of the sliding glass door one of Ivy's toy poodles yapping and scratching at the glass, trying to get to Hayley.

Was it Sneezy?

Or Doc?

Who cared? He was about to give away her position. She tried silently shooing him away but he wasn't going anywhere. In fact, his incessant barking drew the attention of the other six dogs and within seconds they were all at the glass door jumping and yelping and spinning around in circles.

Nykki stood up from her chaise lounge, curious about what had gotten them so riled up, and gasped in surprise when she spotted Hayley squatting behind the potted plant.

"I should've known it would be you," Nykki sneered, shaking her head.

Hayley sheepishly climbed to her feet, brushing the potted soil off her knees.

"I rang the bell twice but nobody answered," she said.

Sabrina dropped her glass of spiked lemonade and it smashed against the wooden floor of the deck.

"Most people would take that as a sign that either no one was home or they weren't welcome," Nykki said, glaring at her for a moment before glancing back to check on Sabrina, who was a cowering mess in her chaise lounge. "May I ask what you're doing here?"

"I came to check on Nigel just to see how he's doing," Hayley stammered, knowing they would never believe her.

"Well, Nigel is at the police station being questioned by Chief Alvares right now," Nykki said.

"What did you hear, Hayley?" Sabrina blurted out in a panic.

Nykki spun around. "Sabrina, why don't you go

inside and get some rest? I know you're still upset about Ivy's murder."

"She was right there! She must have heard something," Sabrina cried, her voice quivering.

"Seriously, Sabrina, go inside. And be careful of the broken glass. We don't need you cutting your foot."

Nykki's tone was direct enough that Sabrina finally clammed up, gingerly stepped around the broken glass and wet wood from the spilled cocktail, and then bolted inside the cottage, pushing the dogs back with her leg before shutting the glass door.

Nykki patiently waited until she was gone before she addressed Hayley again. "Why don't you come back another time when it's more convenient?"

"Nykki, whatever is going on between you two, you can tell me."

Nykki smiled.

There was no way she was going to talk.

Hayley figured it was worth a shot.

Something distracted Nykki, who stared past Hayley and down the path to the shore. Hayley turned to see Mason Cassidy, in a tight blue speedo, emerge from the surf, having gone for an afternoon swim in the ocean. His taut tattooed muscles glistened in the sunlight, and as he trudged out of the surf shaking the water out of his hair and wiping the sea salt from his eyes, it was hard not to appreciate his sheer manly ruggedness and action hero swagger.

Nykki turned back to Hayley. "In case you're

not aware, he's unavailable, Hayley, so for Sabrina's sake please make a note of it."

"I'm not interested in Mason."

"Really? You certainly have a funny way of showing it."

"That kiss you saw at the reunion. I didn't ask for it. I didn't want it."

Nykki nodded. "Okay. Thanks for stopping by, Hayley."

"I'd really like to explain what happened to Sabrina myself."

"You have nothing to worry about. I never mentioned what I saw to her."

"Why not?"

"Because it's none of my business."

"Then what were two talking so intently about right before Ivy was murdered?"

"And that, my dear, is none of *your* business."

Nykki then pivoted toward the sliding glass door, her back to Hayley, and marched inside, stopping only to shove three of Ivy's yapping dogs out of her way with a firm kick.

She slammed the glass door shut.

By now, Mason had spotted Hayley, and with a lascivious look on his face, he bounded up the gravel path from the beach to join her on the porch.

There was no way she was going to wait for him. Before he had a chance to reach her, she dashed back around the side of the house to her car parked out front, jumped in the driver's seat and sped away.

Chapter 14

"I'm working on the Ivy Foster high school reunion murder story and I've come up with a great title. *Most Likely to Succeed . . . with Murder!*" Bruce Linney said, poking his head out into the front office where Hayley worked at her computer at her desk.

"I'm sorry, what?" Hayley said, not sure she heard him correctly.

"Maybe I should go with something simpler and more to the point. Like *Class Reunion Killer!*"

"Bruce, what the hell are you talking about?"

"You know I've been toying with the idea of writing my first true crime book. Let's face it, I've been wasting away as a small town crime reporter long enough. It's time to expand my horizons, focus on the big picture, and when your friend got whacked at your reunion, I thought to myself, this is it. This is my ticket to stardom as a bestselling author and maybe even the host of my own reality show on Investigation Discovery. I've certainly got the looks for it. Plenty of women have told me that."

Hayley's jaw nearly dropped to the floor.

She took a moment to collect herself, and then stood up and slowly walked over to Bruce.

She stared at him, her eyes fixed on his.

Bruce took a half step back, a bit uncomfortable with how much she was invading his personal space.

Hayley stepped forward and closed the gap, and then without warning, she slapped Bruce hard across the face.

So hard she left a red mark on his cheek.

"Jesus, Hayley! What the hell did you do that for?"

"You sick bastard! How dare you even consider taking advantage of my friend's death just to further your own dismally pathetic career!"

"Well, man, when you put it like that, it makes me sound kind of insensitive," Bruce said, rubbing the side of his throbbing face.

"Kind of? Bruce, you should hear yourself. You sound almost gleeful that one of my former classmates is dead."

"Come on. It's not my fault somebody beat her brains out at the reunion. I'm not a monster, Hayley. I mean, I do feel bad for her husband and her family and everybody who knew her. I'm just saying, her death shouldn't be in vain. Perhaps there is some good that can come of it."

"You getting your own TV show?"

"No. But a book about the murder, written by a

trained professional with an up-close and personal view of the case, could go a long way in helping to bring her killer to justice. Lots of murderers got away with it because the police missed a clue in the initial investigation but then were caught after a book was written that revealed a lost detail that finally led to an arrest."

Hayley shook her head.

Could this guy get any worse?

"The TV show is just an added bonus," Bruce said casually.

Yes.

He could.

"Get out of my sight, Bruce. I don't want you even near me right now."

"Oh, Hayley, lighten up. It's not like you were actually close to the victim. I heard you complaining about her and the other two to Liddy and Mona on the phone at least a dozen times before the reunion."

"So now you're eavesdropping on my phone calls?"

"I'm an investigative reporter. It's my job to keep my eyes and ears open."

"Ivy's death is a tragedy. Not an opportunity for you to exploit," Hayley said, her voice low and threatening enough for Bruce to back away from her toward the office bullpen.

"Why can't it be both?" he squeaked, unable to stop himself.

The phone on Hayley's desk rang.

She scooped up the receiver, grateful she now

had a reason to ignore Bruce. "*Island Times*, this is Hayley."

"It's Sergio. Am I getting you at a bad time?"

"No, Sergio. Your timing is impeccable. You better get down here right away and arrest me for assault."

"It was just a slap," Bruce said.

"That was just the beginning," Hayley warned, scowling. "I can do a hell of a lot more damage in the five minutes it will take him to drive over here."

Bruce folded his arms and grimaced, but did not retreat. He was too curious as to why the chief of police was calling Hayley. It could be a family matter, but he was betting it was about the Ivy Foster case.

And he was right.

"I spent the whole day questioning Ivy Foster's husband Nigel. I could barely understand a word he was saying because his accent was so thick," Sergio said in a thick Brazilian accent.

"He's English," Hayley said.

"And I thought the American accent was hard to understand. Anyway, he admitted to having a public fight with his wife just before she was killed, but denied there were problems in the marriage. Should I believe him?" Sergio asked.

Hayley was about to answer, but then noticed Bruce hovering in the doorway, listening to her every word as he pretended to flip through the latest issue of the paper.

"Sergio, let me call you back on my cell."

Hayley slammed down the phone and then grabbed her bag from underneath the desk and stormed out the front door. "I"m taking my break, Bruce!"

Bruce hurled the paper to the floor in frustration as Hayley left the building. She walked around the corner of the building to make doubly sure Bruce was well out of earshot before fishing her cell phone out of the bag and calling back Sergio. He picked up on the first ring.

"Chief Alvares," he said.

"He's lying, Sergio. I know for a fact they had a strained marriage. She was berating and embarrassing him from the moment I met him. It was tough to watch."

"Do you think she might have driven him to the boiling point?"

"Breaking point. I'm not sure. She rode him really hard. But I don't know if that was enough to send him into a murderous rage and bludgeon her to death!"

"Maybe it wasn't a crime of passion. Maybe it was more calibrated."

"Calculated."

"What?"

"Never mind. Why do you say that?"

"Because I did a little digging and I found out that Nigel *just* took out a big life insurance policy on his wife Ivy two weeks ago. He signed the papers two days before they got on a plane in New York to fly up here for the reunion."

Hayley fell back against the brick wall of the office building, stunned.

Things suddenly looked very bad for Ivy's hen-pecked British-born husband.

She then noticed Bruce hanging out his office window a few feet away from her, straining to hear any snippets of her conversation with Sergio.

She flipped him the finger before marching back around to the front of the building.

Chapter 15

"I am not, do you hear me, *not* going to bury my wife in a pink box!" Nigel roared in the casket selection room of McFarland's Funeral Home.

"But it's the same color as the frosting on her most popular cupcakes," a woman who vaguely resembled the deceased countered. "I personally believe it would be a fitting tribute!"

"It costs twelve hundred dollars!"

"I can't believe you're penny pinching on your own wife's funeral, Nigel," the woman huffed. "You may have a posh English accent, but you are decidedly low class."

Hayley stood just outside the selection room, trying to remain inconspicuous. She had stopped by McFarland's on her way home from the office to see the funeral home owner, Lacey, with whom she had gone to high school. Lacey had recently taken over running the business since her parents were retiring and moving to Florida. Hayley needed Lacey to sign off on an ad that was to be placed in next Monday's paper. There was a discrepancy about whether an exterior shot of the building or an interior shot of the main visitation room was to be featured and instead of e-mailing back and forth Hayley thought it would be easier just to drop in and take care of the matter in person on her way home.

Lacey was busy in the arrangement room with an elderly woman grieving the recent loss of her husband, so Hayley waited in the hallway. She had only been there a few seconds before she heard Nigel arguing with a woman Hayley assumed was Ivy's sister, Irene, who was a few years younger and had just flown in from California to help with arrangements. She hadn't seen her since they were kids, but the two sisters shared similar features and both had the same irritating high-pitched squealing voice.

"I was thinking more along the lines of this one," Nigel said abruptly.

"You've got to be kidding! You might as well stuff her body in a garbage bag and leave it out on the street!" Irene wailed.

"Don't be so overdramatic, Irene, it's a perfectly fine casket."

"What is it called, the welfare casket? It looks like it's made of cheap plywood! It doesn't even have an adjustable head rest like this one over here."

"Ivy's not going to care about comfort! She's dead!"

"My God, I knew you were cold, Nigel, but this is horrific behavior even for you!"

Nigel took a deep breath. "Let's just get through this, shall we?"

"Fine. If you're too cheap to bury my sister in a proper last resting place then I'll pay for it. We're going with the pink one. Any objections?"

Nigel threw his hands up in the air, surrendering. "Whatever you want, Irene."

Lacey McFarland hurried out of the office in a smart gray pants suit. She was stocky with close-cropped blond hair and normally a big inviting smile, but today she was in business mode and kept her face a mask of seriousness and empathy.

When she spotted Hayley, she couldn't resist letting her lovely smile creep back.

"Hayley, I haven't seen you in ages," Lacey said, before quickly wiping the smile off her face. "You're not here on business, are you? I mean, nobody's passed to the other side, I hope!"

"Oh, lord no; I'm just here to go over your ad for the *Island Times*."

"What a relief! Let me just finish up in there and then we can chat," Lacey said, clasping her hands together and affixing her concerned, caring funeral director's expression on her face before hustling into the selection room. "Have we made any decisions?"

"Yes, we will take the Persian Rose Deluxe Slumber Chamber with the velvet bedding and adjustable head rest and I also want to buy the guaranteed one hundred year termite protection warranty," Irene said. "I will be the one paying for it."

"Very well. Shall we go to my office and fill out the paperwork?"

"Yes. And just so you know, Ms. McFarland, I will be handling all the other arrangements as well. I'm afraid if we leave the details to Ivy's husband, my poor sister will wind up just propped up on a couch for the viewing."

"Certainly, Irene. Come with me. And let me say again, I am so, so sorry for your loss, both of you."

"Just make sure Irene doesn't drag this circus out. I want the service and burial as close together as possible. The sooner I get back to New York, the better," Nigel spit out.

There was an awkward silence.

Lacey then came around the corner guiding Irene to her office with a gentle hand underneath her arm.

Irene didn't acknowledge Hayley.

She was too busy dabbing her eye with a wadded up Kleenex.

Lacey, however, nodded to Hayley and mouthed, "Be right with you."

They disappeared into the office and shut the door just as Nigel barreled around the corner and nearly slammed into Hayley.

"Oh, hello," he said in his clipped English accent.

"Nigel, we met at the golf club shortly after you and Ivy arrived in town," Hayley said, quietly. "I'm Hayley. I went to high school with—"

"I know who you are," Nigel said.

"I just want to say how sorry I am . . ."

"You can stop being nice. I know you and all of Ivy's friends think I did it. That I couldn't take Ivy's verbal abuse anymore and I just snapped."

"I don't necessarily think that . . ."

"Then you're the only one."

"I was hoping we could talk . . ."

"I'm not interested in sitting down and remembering all the good times with Ivy, and even if I was, we'd be done in less than a minute so let's not waste each other's time."

Nigel's cell phone rang. He fumbled around looking for it before finally locating it in the breast pocket of his tweed jacket. He checked the caller ID. His eyes widened slightly before he glanced over at Hayley and pressed the screen against his chest, worried she might get a glimpse of the name flashing on his phone.

"I need to take this. Excuse me," Nigel said, brushing past her and clamping the phone to his ear as he headed toward the door.

Hayley heard him say in a hushed whisper. "I can't talk right now. I'm going outside. Hang on."

He cranked his head around to see if Hayley was watching him but she managed to look the other way pretending not to care.

Satisfied, he shoved open the door and hot-footed it outside.

But Hayley did care.

She wanted to know who Nigel was so desperate to talk to without any eavesdroppers around.

If the man did kill his wife, was it possible he had some kind of help doing it?

Chapter 16

His flexing muscles glistened with sweat as he waved the electric trimmer over the top of the hedge. He wiped some perspiration off his brow and adjusted the baseball cap he was wearing to keep the blazing sun out of his eyes, which was just now retreating below the ocean's horizon in the late hours of the afternoon. He was shirtless, his smooth chest and torso truly a sight to behold. And he was completely oblivious he was being stared at by a group gathered around a picnic table close to the main house on the property where he had been hired to work.

Hayley watched with a smile as Gemma completely missed her mouth with a forkful of crabmeat salad because she was so drawn to the masculine image of perfection so close to her. Some mayo dribbled down the front of her Rock the Vote t-shirt and she reached for a napkin to clean her cheek.

Dustin snorted and shook his head then went

back to gnawing at his corn on the cob stopping only when a tiny kernel got wedged between his teeth.

Gemma tried acting casual but it was to no avail. "Who's that?"

Randy touched his husband Sergio's arm before pretending to notice the young man working near the edge of the property close to the path that led to the rocky shore line. "Oh, him? That's Hardy. Our new gardener."

"He's cute," Gemma said nonchalantly, but failing miserably. She tried again to put some crabmeat in her mouth but it proved too challenging to stare and eat at the same time so she threw her fork down.

"He usually comes on Sundays, but I told him we needed our hedges trimmed today."

"Why? They look fine," Hayley said.

"They are. I evened the tops yesterday myself, but then I remembered my gorgeous niece was coming over this evening for a family barbecue, and I thought, "Wouldn't it be nice for the two of them to meet? Who knows? They might hit it off. He's just back from his freshman year at Bates College."

"Good school," Hayley said.

"I wouldn't fix my favorite niece up with just anyone," Randy sniffed.

"This is a fix up? And for the record, I'm your only niece. What did you tell him, Uncle Randy?"

"I told him the truth about you," Randy said.

"How could you do that? That's the worst thing you could do!"

"What? Tell him you're beautiful and funny and charming and one hundred percent take after me?"

"I am so embarrassed right now! Nobody look at him! He'll know we're talking about him!" Gemma said, slumping down on the picnic table bench and staring at the grass.

"I thought if the two of you hit it off, you might consider inviting him to be your date for your prom," Randy shrugged.

Gemma whipped around to glare at her mother. "You told him I got dumped by Nate Forte?"

"He asked who you were going with and I may have mentioned what happened," Hayley said. "What's the big deal?"

"What's the big deal? This! This is the big deal! You didn't think Uncle Randy would pull something like this?"

"FYI, I'm sitting right here," Randy huffed. "What's so wrong with trying to help you find a date? I said to your mother that there was no reason you should be stuck choosing from the pool of boys in your graduating class. The key to a hot date is casting a wider net."

"I just want to shrink until I disappear right now," Gemma said, hunched over. "I am so humiliated."

"Should I call him over?" Randy asked.

"Is this some weird version of that old *Sixth Sense* movie? Have I somehow died and I'm now a ghost that no one can hear? Please don't *do* or *say* anything! I'm begging you."

"Fine. We'll change the subject," Randy said, scooping some leafy salad onto his plate from a wooden bowl. "Dustin, are you excited for summer vacation?"

"I flunked my history final and now they want me to go to summer school to make up for it or they're going to hold me back a year," Dustin said quickly as he chewed on his corn. "I'm done. Who's next?"

"Wait. Back up. What?" Hayley said, turning to her son, a stern look on her face. "When were you going to tell me this?"

"I don't know. Now seemed like a good time. Hey, Uncle Sergio, how's your murder investigation going? Any arrests yet?"

"We're not done with you, Mister," Hayley said wrenching the half eaten corn cob out of Dustin's hand and setting it down on his plate.

Dustin looked at Randy, annoyed. "It didn't work, Uncle Randy."

"What?" Randy said.

"You said the way to get Mom off a subject you don't want to talk about is to mention one of Uncle Sergio's murder cases. It would distract her like a baby watching one of those hanging crib mobiles."

"Oh, really?" Hayley said, shifting in her seat to confront her brother.

"I don't think I ever said that," Randy said half-heartedly, obviously lying. "Or at least I didn't use those exact words."

"There is nothing much to say about it anyway," Sergio said. "I am focusing the investigation on Ivy Foster's husband Nigel, but I have three eyewitnesses who swear he was nowhere near the kitchen when she was killed."

"Most of the guests at the reunion were in plain view at the time Charles McNally discovered the body. Who are we not thinking about?" Hayley said, suddenly distracted.

Dustin grinned from ear to ear as Randy picked up a napkin and hurled it at his nephew's face.

Hayley spun around in an instant and intercepted the napkin, rubbing some greasy butter off her son's face. "Don't think for a minute we're done talking about that history final."

"I'm pretty much done with the hedges. Anything else you'd like trimmed before I leave?" Hardy said, surprising everyone with his stealth arrival at the table.

"Uh, no, that's it, Hardy," Randy said, fumbling. "By the way, have you met my niece Gemma?"

"Hi," Hardy said, revealing a mega watt grin and dimples.

Gemma shuddered and nodded her head. "Hey, how's it going?"

"Isn't she a beauty?" Randy said as Gemma kicked him hard under the table and he flinched.

"Very pretty," Hardy agreed.

There was an interminable amount of silence before Dustin stuck his hand out. "I'm Dustin. The ignored nephew."

Hardy chuckled and shook his hand. "Hardy. Nice to meet you, Dustin."

"And that's my stunningly beautiful mother with a sparkling personality," Dustin said, waving an arm at Hayley.

"Sweet words are not going to make me forget about you going to summer school," Hayley said, eyes narrowing.

"Then let me rephrase that. That's my mother," Dustin said, giving up.

"Gemma, have you found a dress for your prom yet?" Randy asked innocently.

Gemma stared at him.

She could not believe this was happening.

"Yes, Uncle Randy. I have. But I'm thinking about not going at all."

"But it's your senior prom. You have to go. It would be a crying shame if you didn't. Wouldn't it, Hardy?"

"Oh, yeah. I had a blast at mine last year," Hardy said.

"Hardy went to high school in Waterville. He's just down here for the summer gardening to help pay for college," Randy said.

Gemma squirmed in her seat, wanting to die.

"You have most nights free though, right?" Randy asked.

"Most of them, yeah."

"Hey, I have a wild idea," Randy said, acting as if a lightbulb just went off in his head.

"Uncle Randy, please!" Gemma said, almost bawling.

"Never mind, Hardy. I shouldn't interfere," Randy said, calculating his response.

"No. What is it?" Hardy said, curious.

Gemma, ashen-faced, eyes afire, picked up a butter knife and wielded it menacingly at her uncle.

Randy finally took the hint. "It was just a crazy thought. Forget it."

Gemma sat up straight and sighed with relief.

"He was going to ask if you would take Gemma to her prom next weekend," Dustin said, gleefully jumping at the chance to embarrass his sister.

Gemma tried hard not to leap across the picnic table and strangle him.

"I would love to," Hardy said.

Everyone took a collective breath.

"But unfortunately Robin's coming to the island next weekend for a visit."

"Who's Robin? Your girlfriend?" Hayley asked.

"No. My boyfriend."

"What? I had no idea you were gay," Randy said, flabbergasted.

"Really? That's funny. I knew right away you were."

Hayley guffawed, spitting out her lemonade.

"If it was any other weekend, I'd be honored to escort you, Gemma," Hardy said, winking. "Better go find my shirt."

Hardy ambled off toward the house.

"Well, that went well," Hayley said.

"I am going to focus on how much I love you so I don't kill you, Uncle Randy," Gemma said. "But you should definitely know that I will, I am not sure when or how, but I *will* get even with you for that disgraceful display!"

"Just trying to help," Randy said. "I had so much fun at my prom that I just want you to experience that same kind of memory."

"Who did you go with, Uncle Randy?" Dustin asked, reaching for another corn on the cob before snatching the butter knife out of Gemma's hand, scooping up some butter and slathering it all over its side.

"Lori O'Malley. She was my best friend and beard for both eighth grade and senior prom. She knew I was gay but didn't care because we always had such a good time hanging out together."

"Did you ever have a boyfriend when you were a kid?" Sergio asked, finally deciding to join the conversation because the topic was finally interesting him.

"Oh God, no! I was too much of a closet case! Though it was no secret to anybody since I spent the entire second grade running around playing Charlie's Angels and karate chopping all the boys I had crushes on."

"Not even in high school?" Dustin asked.

"By then, I considered myself too sophisticated to settle for a townie. I set my sights higher. I was saving myself for George Michael. Then there was Julian Reed. Remember him, Hayley?"

"How could I forget? He rented a house here on the island one summer years ago."

"Who is Julian Reed? I never heard of him," Sergio said.

"He was an actor. Kind of the Rob Lowe of his day. Very sexy. More beautiful than most of the women he dated. I wore out my VHS copy of *Summer Fling* where he was the pool boy at the country club who got involved with some billionaire's daughter and the family didn't think he was good enough for her, and they wind up running away together and he gets shot in the end by the girl's father and it looks like he's going to die but his love proves too strong and he recovers and rescues her from that private school that's like a girls' prison."

"Looks like we can skip watching it on Netflix," Gemma said.

"I'm assuming his career died right after that," Dustin said.

"No," Randy said. "He did. Right here on the island."

Sergio, Gemma, and Dustin all perked up, suddenly interested.

"Remember, Hayley?"

"How could I forget? It was right after my high school graduation."

"He got blisteringly drunk one night that summer and fell and hit his head on the cement and drowned in his swimming pool. It was so tragic. Such a waste."

"I remember you were so shook up over it because you idolized him and you mourned his death that whole summer," Hayley said.

"I was obsessed with him. Ever since he did that *Cosmo* spread totally nude. Well, not totally nude, he had a throw pillow over his junk. But he was so freaking hot and the second I heard about it I knew I had to get a copy but I was deathly afraid someone would see me buying it so I shoplifted one from Carey's Corner Store."

"Yeah, and Mom found it in your room and I covered for you and told her it was mine."

"Thanks for that, by the way. I still have my copy if you want to see it, Hayley," Randy said.

"I do! I want to see it!" Sergio blurted out as if he didn't realize he was talking out loud.

They all laughed.

Even Gemma.

And Hayley knew her daughter would find it in her heart to forgive her overly helpful uncle.

But that still didn't solve the problem of her daughter's broken heart.

Or the identity of Ivy Foster's killer.

Island Food & Spirits
by
Hayley Powell

The other night, while sipping a delicious summer lemonade cocktail I had just made, Mona stopped by and gave me a basket full of lemons from the tree in her yard. She usually handed them out to her customers at her seafood shop, but this week she had picked too many so I benefited from her leftovers. I decided to whip up a lemon tart, always a summer party favorite.

I ran out to the garage to grab a couple of boxes of puff pastry that I always keep on hand in my chest freezer. Much to my surprise, the garage was spotless. I usually moan and groan at the messy piles of junk, but today it looked downright orderly. That certainly wasn't the case a couple of months ago.

Last winter I was forced to have a

new roof put on the garage when an unfortunate pileup of snow on the old roof caused it to cave in. So, with a sturdy new roof, my kids deemed the garage a suitable place for them to toss all of their unwanted old toys, books, games, bags of clothes, and anything else they didn't want in their rooms but refused to throw away. This was on top of the already stored bikes, rollerblades, sleds, wagons, and skis that were piled up in there.

I would be lying if I didn't admit I was also at fault for the packed garage. I had some boxes of clothes I swore I'd fit into soon stacked in the corner, some stray kitchen items I didn't have room for in my cupboards, and even a pink treadmill. Yes, pink. I know. I know. But it was one of those New Year's resolutions to get back into shape that faded by mid-January and by then I resented having to look at the sponta-neous expensive purchase so I had Aaron help me haul it to the garage so I wouldn't have to look at it. The garage was in such utter chaos there wasn't even room for me to park my car when I got home from work one night. Apparently, Dustin and his friend Spanky had been looking for some of his old superhero action figures and left them in the middle of the garage floor, so I had to park outside to avoid crushing Superman and Green Lantern.

This was the last straw. I marched into the house where my two cherubs were flopped on the couch in the living room watching Doctor Who with snack wrappers and juice bottles strewn all around them. I told them in no uncertain terms that if they ever wanted to see their friends again—if they ever wanted to have any kind of social life outside of the house before they finished high school—they would spend their entire Saturday cleaning out the garage. I had plans to drive up to Bangor with Mona to stock up on some bulk food times (plus we set aside some time to gamble at Hollywood Slots, but I left out that tiny detail while yelling at the kids) and the garage was to be in tip top shape when I returned. I would rent a large garbage bin for the junk and the rest we would donate to Goodwill.

The following morning, the kids got out of bed at the crack of dawn and began carrying out boxes from the garage without argument. Sometimes, a firm hand is exactly what is needed. Mona and I left for Bangor, and by lunchtime we had all our shopping done and were enjoying a couple of hours of mental therapy playing the slot machines.

Unfortunately the noise of the slot machines sometimes drowns out my ringing cell phone, so when Mona and I finished for the day I noticed I had eight missed calls from Liddy. I rang her right back and without even saying hello she immediately started scolding me for not being upfront with her about hating the handpicked hat she had bought me during her trip to Paris last year, and that the polite thing to have done was to at least keep it as a souvenir since God only knows when I would be getting to Paris in the near future. I stood there listening to her tirade.

"Liddy, you've lost me. I have no idea what you're talking about!"

"Your yard sale!"

"What yard sale?"

"Don't you check your Facebook and Twitter feeds? It's all over social media. There was a yard sale at your house from 9 to 3 today."

Gemma and Dustin.

"I happened to swing by the Shop 'n Save to pick up a few necessities," Liddy said.

Wine and cheese, no doubt.

"And I ran into Mrs. Crowley and she was wearing a deep purple felt French hat with a lovely peacock feather sticking out the side. Of course I recognized it immediately! I knew it had to be the one I bought specially for you because I know for a fact old Mrs. Crowley hasn't been past Bangor in her seventy-odd years! That's when she told me she bought it at your yard sale for twenty bucks! Twenty bucks! The box it came in is worth more than that!"

After hanging up with Liddy, Mona and I raced back to the island, passing a small dark blue Toyota Tacoma truck with a bright pink treadmill in the back. My treadmill!

Mona and I glanced at each other, and she hit the gas a little harder as we careened down Spring Street toward Glen Mary Road. I had to admit to myself, I was happy to see that pink treadmill go.

I couldn't believe my eyes when we pulled up to the house. The garage door was wide open and it looked so neat and orderly I thought we had pulled into the wrong driveway!

Well, as much as I wanted to be mad at my kids for selling our property without telling me, I was actually relieved to finally be able to move around in my garage. Plus, the three hundred bucks we split three ways was an added bonus.

Liddy showed up with the purple hat with the peacock feather. I feared she might have wrestled it away from Mrs. Crowley, but she said she paid her thirty dollars for it so the old woman was content with a ten dollar profit. I had to fake my gratitude that she got my hat back even though I knew I would never wear it and it would be sold in the next yard sale.

I fixed us girls some lemonade cocktails and we sat on the deck enjoying the evening view of my spiffy clean garage.

Summer Lemonade Cocktail

<u>Ingredients:</u>

2 cups club soda
½ cup citrus vodka
½ cup fresh lemon juice
¼ cup sugar
¼ cup orange juice
Ice
Lemon slices to garnish (optional)

Put ice in glasses; mix together all five ingredients in a pitcher. Pour in ice filled glasses. Garnish with lemon slices if desired and sit back, relax and bottoms up!

Lemon Tart

<u>Ingredients:</u>

1 sheet puff pastry
2 lemons
Zest of 2 lemons
¾ cup sugar
4 tablespoons butter
2 eggs
¼ lemon juice (from the 2 lemons)
Pinch of salt

Preheat your oven to 450 degrees.

Place your rolled out puff pastry on a parchment lined baking sheet. Fold all sides of pastry in one inch and prick all over with a fork. Bake 20 minutes or until golden brown.

In a food processor add your sugar and the zest of two lemons and pulse until finely minced.

In a bowl cream your butter then add the lemon and sugar mixture, add eggs one at a time mixing in each one, add lemon juice and salt and mix well.

Pour into a 2 quart sauce pan and heat on low until thickened, stirring constantly.

When thickened place into the refrigerator for 1 hour to cool.

Spread cooled mixture on top of the cooked puff pastry slice and serve for a delicious summer treat.

Chapter 17

Liddy pulled her Mercedes into the Congregational Church parking lot and squeezed into the last space between a brand new Range Rover and a five series BMW. "I'm only parking here because it's obvious the owners of these two cars will take extra care not to bang their doors into mine. Otherwise, we'd be parking down the street."

"Wow, I didn't expect such a big crowd," Hayley said, downing a sandwich she had picked up on the way because she didn't have a chance to eat lunch before the service. "I mean, Ivy's lived in New York for years. I didn't realize she still had so many ties to the island."

"Well, it's just a matter of giving the people what they want," Mona said, chuckling from the back seat.

"This is not a joke, Mona. A woman has died. A woman we've known since childhood."

"I'm sorry, but I told you I am not going to be a hypocrite. Ivy Foster never gave me the time of day and had no use for me. The only reason I'm here is because her aunt and uncle who live in Tremont are nice folks and loyal customers of mine, so I'm here out of respect to them."

"Well, just try and behave during the actual service," Liddy said as she whipped open the driver's door and banged the side of the Range Rover. "Oops."

Hayley popped the last of her sandwich in her mouth and crumpled up the wrapping paper in her hands.

"Try not to get crumbs on the upholstery, okay, Hayley?" Liddy warned.

"Yes, Liddy. I'm glad to see you have your priorities in order today," Hayley said, shaking her head.

As Hayley carefully climbed out of the car making sure not to make contact with the BMW with the passenger side door, she spotted Sabrina Merryweather, in a smart, form-fitting black business suit, appropriate for mourning, standing around the side of the church engaged in a conversation with Vanda Spears, who had parked a rusted shopping cart off to the side and wore a lumpy gray sweater and a stained flower print skirt. She looked like a bag lady as she waved her finger in Sabrina's horrified face.

Mona huffed and puffed as she tried squeezing her way out of the backseat since there was very little room to maneuver between the parked cars.

"Liddy, why don't you and Mona go inside and

get us seats. I'll be right in," Hayley said, keeping her eyes fixed on Sabrina and Vanda.

"She's right, Liddy. I bet it's standing room only at this point. They could've sold tickets."

"Mona, enough with the jokes, please!" Hayley scolded. "It's not funny."

Mona shrugged and followed Liddy inside while Hayley quietly tiptoed over to the side of the church toward Sabrina and Vanda, who were too involved in their heated exchange to notice her.

"The last thing you want to do, Sabrina, is upset me because when I get upset I tend to go a little crazy and when I get crazy, I talk. I talk about everything. I get it all off my chest and that could be very uncomfortable for you!" Vanda threatened, sneering at Sabrina.

"Vanda, please, I'm begging you, don't breathe a word. I promise to make things easier for you than they have been. You just have to trust me and not go off blabbing to anyone what you know."

"I'll think about it," Vanda said, moving behind her grocery cart and starting to push it away.

Sabrina shoved her black high heel in front of it, slamming it down on a loose wheel and stopping Vanda in her tracks. "I need you to promise me right now."

Vanda cackled. "Why should I do that? Half the fun for me is watching you squirm. Now get your damn heel off my wheel before I call a cop!"

Sabrina instantly pulled her foot back and Vanda pushed past her, whistling the tune to "I

Got the Music in Me" as Sabrina watched her go, terrified.

Vanda passed by Hayley with her cart. "Afternoon, Hayley. Beautiful day, isn't it?"

"Yes. Nice to see you, Vanda," Hayley said, watching Sabrina who spun around, surprised at Hayley's presence.

"Hayley, would you please stop sneaking around trying to overhear my private conversations? Enough is enough."

"I would if you would just be honest with me. What the hell is going on between you and Vanda Spears?"

"Nothing. She's crazy. She's spewing nonsense. She shouldn't be wandering the streets. She should be locked up in a mental facility."

"That would certainly take care of whatever problem she's causing you," Hayley said, staring at Sabrina.

"I don't know what you're talking about," Sabrina said, blowing past Hayley and racing toward the front entrance of the church.

Hayley followed.

Inside the church, Sabrina managed to ditch Hayley and join a crowd of former high school classmates who were huddled in a corner.

As Hayley scanned the main room for Liddy and Mona, Nykki approached her.

"Can you believe this has happened, Hayley? I am just so distraught!" Nykki wailed as she grabbed Hayley in a bear hug.

When she finally let go, Hayley noticed that despite Nykki's sobs her eyes were completely dry.

No sign of any tears.

It was as if she were putting on a performance.

Which didn't surprise Hayley because it seemed Nykki was always acting.

"Have you seen Liddy and Mona?" Hayley asked.

"Yes," Nykki said, clearing her throat, pretending to pull herself together. "They're down in the front pew. They were the only seats left."

Hayley wasn't happy about sitting in the front row at any funeral. She always felt too exposed. It made her supremely uncomfortable. But it wasn't like she had much of a choice.

She passed Nigel, whose back was to her. He was in his signature tweed jacket that screamed "I am an author!" and had his cell phone clamped to his ear.

"I find it inexcusable that your airline is charging me a change fee for my reservation because I want to go home a day early. My beloved wife has died! Where is your compassion? I am a Premier Silver member and I find your tone grossly inappropriate given these grim circumstances," Nigel barked, seemingly unconcerned that several of Ivy's family members, including her sister Irene, were within earshot.

Hayley couldn't believe his cold and insensitive behavior, but just bit her lip to refrain from commenting.

Suddenly she felt someone's hand cupping her butt and then squeezing the flesh.

She knew who it was.

Hayley whirled around and found herself face to face with Mason Cassidy, most of his body tattoos covered by a crisp linen charcoal gray suit and a white dress shirt that was open enough to show a bit of an eagle's wing tattoo on his tan bronzed chest.

"Well, hello, beautiful," Mason said, a wolfish grin on his face.

"Get your hand off me," Hayley warned, her voice a low growl.

"It's tragic Ivy's dead and all, but we're not," Mason said, defiantly leaving his large hand on Hayley's butt.

Hayley kept a thin smile on her face as she reached behind her and grabbed Mason's hand, bending the fingers back so far he almost dropped to his knees in pain. "I like men, not boys."

She finally let go and he rubbed his fingers, a scowl on his face.

Hayley did an about face and marched down the aisle spotting Liddy and Mona in the far left pew directly in front of a closed coffin.

The coffin.

She got her first look at Ivy's coffin.

Bright pink.

With a giant ceramic cupcake on top.

Instead of flowers there were trays and trays of freshly baked cupcakes surrounding the casket.

Someone had gone way overboard.

Hayley found herself biting her lip again but this time to keep herself from laughing.

How was it possible that the family allowed this embarrassing display to be approved?

Hayley glanced over at Liddy and Mona, who refused to make eye contact with her out of fear of losing their composure and screaming with laughter.

Hayley sat down between her two best friends, now biting the side of her lip so hard she feared drawing blood.

Reverend Staples solemnly walked up the steps and behind the podium. The murmurs faded until there was silence and then he proceeded. "Ivy Foster was a daughter, wife, sister, and master baker. She leaves us with many happy memories of our time with her, not to mention an artistic mark when it comes to her world famous cupcakes. Who could forget her Dark Chocolate Cupcakes with Peanut Butter frosting or my personal favorite her Guinness, Whiskey and Irish Cream cupcakes? More than one and I would need a designated driver to get home from the church."

There were soft titters from the crowd.

"I remember one Christmas my wife bought a box of Ivy's special Santa Claus cupcakes where Santa's beard was made of coconut. Good times. Good times."

Hayley tried desperately not to lose it.

She shifted in her seat.

Covered her mouth with her hand.

She felt her cheeks burning red as she tried to stay calm and composed.

"Ivy Foster's creations were confection perfection," Reverend Staples said. "She was the Monet of her time but she did not use a canvas and paint. No. Her tools were a baking pan and buttercream frosting."

That was it.

Hayley couldn't contain herself any longer.

Without warning a loud guffaw erupted out of her.

Reverend Staples glared down at the front row of the pew where Mona and Liddy kept their eyes glued to the floor while Hayley's entire body shook while wedged between them.

She hugged herself in a last ditch attempt to hold everything inside.

But it was too late.

Her mouth ripped open and a machine gun burst of laughter escaped.

Chapter 18

Hayley didn't know what to do.

She couldn't just jump up and run out of the church because she would have to dash down the center of the aisle for all to see her red-faced and laughing.

Liddy quickly rummaged through her bag for a handkerchief, which Hayley snatched out of her fingers and covered her face with, desperately trying to make it appear as if her fit of giggles were in fact tears of grief.

But nobody was buying it.

Reverend Staples continued to stare down at her from the podium for a few more seconds before resuming his speech. "Ivy baked with love. Her husband Nigel told me a sweet story. He woke up one morning with a cupcake waiting for him on the nightstand next to his side of the bed. A tradition Ivy carried on until Nigel was diagnosed with Type 2 Diabetes."

A loud chortling sound escaped Hayley's lips.

She was losing it again.

Mona, who was never one to be embarrassed, forcefully nudged Hayley in the ribs trying to get her to settle down.

Reverend Staples cleared his throat. "Now I would like to bring up one of Ivy's dearest friends, Sabrina Merryweather, who will be saying a few words."

Sabrina, who was sitting near the back, slowly got to her feet and calmly walked down the aisle and up the steps, offering Reverend Staples a thin smile as he moved aside and let her take over at the podium.

Sabrina's hands were shaking and her mascara was smudged from crying. She scanned the crowd of mourners, took a deep breath, and said, "I first met Ivy when we were both in the third grade. Her family had just moved to Bar Harbor from New Jersey because her Dad had gotten a job as a park ranger in Acadia National Park. On her first day, Mrs. Cook gave us a spelling test and we had to exchange papers with the student next to us when it was time to go over the answers so they could mark the ones we got wrong. That way, nobody could erase their wrong answers and quickly scribble in the correct ones."

There was gentle laughter from the crowd.

Hayley seized the opportunity to laugh along with everybody else.

It was an enormous relief to let it all out and not try to hold it inside anymore.

"I knew I had misspelled seven words," Sabrina

said. "But when Ivy gave me my paper back I had all the right answers. Ivy had changed all my wrong answers to the right ones so I didn't fail the test."

Liddy leaned over to Hayley. "I certainly didn't expect a pro-cheating story."

"We were best friends from that day forward. We'd have slumber parties at each other's houses where we would braid each other's hair and watch scary movies and pop popcorn and tell each other our deepest, darkest secrets," Sabrina said, smiling at the distant memories.

"Why don't you share one of them?" a voice called out from the back of the room.

Everyone turned around to see who was speaking.

In the back of the church, Vanda Spears stood there, scratching her butt with one hand while waving away a curious fly with the other.

Sabrina froze, not sure how to respond.

Vanda wiped her mouth, not taking her eyes off Sabrina except for the two seconds she punched at the air trying to take out the offending fly. "Come on, Sabrina. Tell us one of your secrets that you and Ivy have been keeping all these years."

Sabrina fumbled nervously.

Most of the crowd turned back around in their seats expectantly, waiting to see what Sabrina would do.

"Don't keep us in suspense!" Vanda taunted.

There were now murmurs from the crowd.

Liddy turned to Mona. "Mona, do something."

"What do I look like, some kind of big, bruising bouncer?" Mona scoffed.

"As a matter of fact, you do," Liddy said.

Reverend Staples finally took charge of the awkward situation and marched down the aisle to escort Vanda out. He gently took her arm and whispered something in her ear but she shook him off.

"We're waiting, Sabrina! Looks like she's drawing a big fat blank," Vanda yelled. "Well, no worries, folks. I got a secret and it's a doozy!"

Sabrina suddenly left the podium, bolting down the steps and out the side door that led to a room where the church served tea and coffee after services.

There was a stunned silence from the crowd.

"Was it something I said?" Vanda asked innocently before settling her gaze on the wide variety of multi-colored cupcakes surrounding Ivy Foster's casket. "Those cupcakes sure look delicious. Mind if I take one for the road?"

Ivy's sister Irene stood up near the front, plucked one off the display next to the coffin and nearly hurled it at Vanda, who bit into it and got butter cream frosting all over her face.

And then, with more forceful urging from Reverend Staples, Vanda Spears finally got the hint that she had worn out her welcome and casually strolled out the door.

Irene ran back down the aisle and knelt down beside Hayley, who had mercifully finally gotten her giggle fit under control. "Hayley, would you mind terribly finishing the eulogy?"

"I'm sorry, what?" Hayley said, coughing.

"We can't just leave people hanging. Someone has to speak."

"What about Nykki? She was much closer to Ivy than I was."

"She left around the time Vanda interrupted the service. You're the only one here who can do it."

"But you're her sister!"

"I have a crippling fear of public speaking. We have other family members speaking, but it's important we hear from one of her close friends. Please, Hayley. I'm begging you!"

As if in a trance, Hayley rose to her feet and walked up to the podium.

She was numb.

What was she going to say?

What if she started laughing again?

She looked out at the somber crowd.

She opened her mouth to speak.

Her hands were shaking more than Sabrina's had been.

Then she felt it rising in her throat.

Oh no!

Don't laugh.

Don't laugh.

For the love of God, don't laugh!

But she didn't laugh.

She suddenly burst into tears, letting out a wail.

The crowd nodded solemnly, moved by Hayley's unabashed show of emotion.

She didn't dare admit they were not actually tears of grief over the loss of Ivy Foster.

They were, in fact, tears of relief.

Yes. She was crying because she was just so immensely relieved that she wasn't laughing.

Reverend Staples walked back down the aisle and joined Hayley behind the podium, putting his hands on her shoulders, his head bowed, consoling her.

Through her sobs, Hayley managed to choke out a few kind words about the deceased.

Talented baker.

Successful businesswoman.

Loyal friend.

She threw that last one in for good measure knowing full well it wasn't true.

But the crowd of mourners seemed to appreciate it and after a few more improvised platitudes Hayley was finally back in her seat.

It was someone else's turn to fib about what a wonderful woman Ivy Foster was.

Chapter 19

"Vanda, wait! Slow down! I need to talk to you!" Hayley screamed, nearly out of breath, as she chased down Vanda on the sidewalk of Ledgelawn Avenue after the Ivy Foster memorial service was over.

Vanda pushed her grocery cart as fast as she could, huffing and puffing, apparently going nowhere in particular since she didn't seem to have a home as far as Hayley knew.

Hayley finally managed to catch up to her. She grabbed a fistful of Vanda's tattered gray wool sweater that was way too warm to be wearing in the June heat.

"I have nothing to say to you, Hayley Powell!" Vanda spit out, blasting a wave of putrid breath into Hayley's face.

Nauseated, Hayley tried to ignore it. "Vanda, you know I'm not like those other women. I was never in their league in high school."

"But you wanted to be and that makes you just

as bad in my book," Vanda said, shaking free of Hayley's grip and then fingering a large moth-eaten hole in the arm of her sweater before swatting at the imaginary fly buzzing around her.

"We all wanted to fit in when we were younger," Hayley said. "You can't still blame me for that."

Vanda sniffed and then wiped her nose with her forefinger before brushing the snot off on her stained flower skirt. She then reached into one of the paper bags that filled her grocery cart and retrieved a crushed box of Snackwell's creme sandwich cookies, tearing through it for a half eaten one that Hayley feared she had fished out of someone's garbage.

"Want one?" Vanda asked.

"No, thanks. I'm good."

"What is it you want, Hayley?"

"I saw you talking to Sabrina outside the church before Ivy's memorial service and she seemed very upset and then of course I was there when you heckled her during her eulogy."

Vanda cackled, enjoying the fact that she had caused such a ruckus. "That was so great, right? I mean, I just love seeing that bitch squirm."

"Vanda, what kind of dirt do you have on Sabrina and Nykki? Why are they so frightened of you? What's this big secret?"

"You really want to know?"

"Yes," Hayley said, leaning in toward Vanda despite her stomach churning body odor.

"It'll cost you five thousand bucks!"

"You know I don't have that kind of money. I'm

raising two kids on my own and one is going to college in the fall."

"Then we got nothing further to talk about."

"You seriously have a secret that's worth that much?"

"I sure as hell do!" Vanda said, chomping down on the creme sandwich cookie and then licking her fingers clean.

Or relatively clean compared to what they were before.

"I can't tell you how satisfying it is having something so big over these rich stuck-up princesses who were so mean to me in high school. There really is such a thing as karma. Back then they made my life miserable. And now, now when I say jump, they jump. It's a beautiful feeling!"

And with that, Vanda Spears spun around and pushed her cart across the street.

Out of the corner of her eye, Hayley spotted a car approaching.

A red sports car of some kind.

The driver hit the accelerator and sped up just as Vanda reached the middle of the street.

The car wasn't slowing down as it barreled right for Vanda, who by now, realized she was about to be mowed down.

She threw her arms up in the air, surprised.

Without thinking, Hayley raced into the street, tackling Vanda. They both hit the pavement with a thud, and with all her strength, Hayley hugged Vanda tightly and rolled to the right. They tumbled over each other until Hayley's back slammed into the curb, nearly cracking it. Vanda was on top of her, pinning her to the ground, her noxious breath a relentless assault on Hayley's nostrils.

Hayley cranked her neck in time to see the red sports car smash into Vanda's shopping cart, hurling it high into the air. It landed on its side, bags and snack food and dirty blankets flying everywhere.

Hayley caught a glimpse of the driver as the car screeched past.

A woman with thick blond wavy hair and dark glasses.

The car sped away leaving a cloud of dust but Hayley managed to catch a quick look at the license plate before it rounded a corner and disappeared, the roar of the engine finally fading away.

She tried memorizing the number.

Maine plate.

27D 3GG.

27D 3GG.

"Vanda, are you all right?" Hayley gasped, her lungs nearly crushing beneath the weight of Vanda's body.

Vanda pushed off Hayley, and used the support of one knee to stand up. One of her smudged nylons she was wearing was torn open and a small trickle of blood ran down a scraped knee.

"Look at what you did to me, Hayley!" Vanda screamed.

"What?"

"I'm bleeding here! How dare you manhandle me like that! I could press charges!"

"I saved your life!"

"There you go again making such a big deal about everything! Just like in high school! No wonder nobody liked you."

"Excuse me?"

Vanda inspected her cart and kicked it, frustrated. "The back wheel came off my cart! I suppose that's not your fault either!"

"Actually I was going to blame the car that came out of nowhere and almost ran you down before I pushed you out of the way."

"So what do you want, the friggin' Medal of Honor?"

Vanda trudged over and sifted through her belongings, which were scattered all over the street.

"Would you like some help picking your things up?" Hayley asked.

"I got it. You've done enough for one day!" Vanda sneered.

Hayley headed back to the church where she hoped Liddy and Mona were still waiting for her.

Vanda's lack of gratitude didn't concern her.

But the license plate of the hit and run car certainly did.

27D 3GG.

27D 3GG.

27-Dustin-3-Gemma-Gemma.

Chapter 20

"The car is registered with a local rental company. I called them and they told me that particular vehicle was rented to Ivy Foster," Sergio said as he handed Hayley the printout in his office at the police station.

Hayley checked the information and then looked at Sergio, who sat behind his desk with his hands clasped behind his head looking very official in his police chief uniform.

"Well, obviously Ivy didn't return from the dead and try to take out Vanda Spears with her rental car, so who was behind the wheel?"

"Her husband Nigel is listed on the rental agreement as an additional driver. Might have been him," Sergio said.

"No. The driver was definitely a woman," Hayley said.

"What about Sabrina?"

"I saw her outside the church with her boy toy Mason when I went back to meet Liddy and Mona.

He was consoling her. There would be no way for her to try and run down Vanda, ditch the car, and make it back to the church before I did."

"What about the other friend?"

"Nykki. When Liddy and I first met Sabrina, Ivy, and Nykki at the golf club to plan the reunion, I remember Ivy letting Nykki borrow her rental car. They're all staying at the same summer house so it makes perfect sense that Nykki would know where Ivy kept the car keys and would have access to the car."

"I should bring her in for questioning."

"But the woman driving the car had blond hair. Nykki's a redhead."

"That's still enough to at least bring her in."

"Let me talk to her first, Sergio. Nykki's a little high strung. To say the least. If you drag her in here, even if she's innocent, she'll probably lawyer up and never talk. Maybe I can find a way to get her to open up. Give me a couple of hours before you send your deputies over there to pick her up."

"Okay. You have until five o'clock. I don't want to be interrogating a suspect too late. It's date night and Randy will kill me if I have to cancel."

Hayley left the police station and drove straight over to the summer rental house in Seal Harbor.

There was no sign of a red sports car.

She parked her Kia in the gravel driveway and crossed to the front door, knocking on it several times.

No answer.

Instead of slinking around back like last time, she chose to simply try the door.

It was unlocked.

Hayley poked her head inside. "Nykki? Sabrina? Anybody home?"

The place was deserted.

Hayley poked around until she came upon what she assumed was Nykki's room because of the Louis Vuitton luggage and a couple of pressed business suits hanging behind the bathroom door.

She surveyed the room for anything out of the ordinary.

She checked the drawers.

Linens.

Towels.

Ladies underwear.

One drawer was locked.

That was odd.

Why was this one particular drawer inaccessible?

Hayley scooted to the living room and found a gold letter opener on a wooden desk next to a small statue of Paul Bunyan, the mythical lumberjack with a double-sided ax slung over his shoulder. It was an exact replica of the 31 foot high version that stood atop a stone pedestal in front of the Bangor Civic Center in Bass Park. The city, claiming to be the birthplace of the lumber industry, boasted that it was the largest statue of Mr. Bunyan in the world. This trinket, however, was roughly the size of an Academy Award but felt almost as heavy as the real one when she picked it up. Hayley silently scolded herself for taking the

time to look at a funny little statue when someone
could walk in on her at any moment. She set it
back down, scooped up the letter opener and returned to Nykki's room where she used it to jam
open the lock. It was an old antique dresser so it
wasn't difficult.

She slid it open and gasped.

A blond wig and dark sunglasses.

It was Nykki.

Nykki was definitely the mad driver who tried to
run down Vanda Spears in Ivy's rental car.

She stepped back, her mind racing.

Then she sat down on the unmade bed to
consider her next move.

Call Sergio and let him know what she found so
he could arrest Nykki.

A pang of guilt gnawed at her.

She was never a fan of Nykki Temple.

But to be the one who uncovered the evidence
that would undoubtedly put her away for a long
time was sobering.

She was about to stand up and pull out her cell
phone when she noticed something on the crin-
kled white bed sheet.

A hair.

A black hair.

And not just one.

There were tons of them.

Spread out everywhere.

Could it be one of Ivy's toy poodles?

No. They wouldn't shed that much.

It was more like a man's body hair.

A very hairy man.

Was Nykki sneaking a man into her room at night?

The hair certainly didn't belong to Nykki.

She was a redhead.

Suddenly, without warning, the whole house filled with an incessant cacophony of high-pitched barking.

The dogs were in the house.

And it took them less than ten seconds to sniff out Hayley's presence before they charged into Nykki's room and surrounded her, yapping and jumping and nipping at her ankles.

Hayley tired to make a fast getaway out the window but only managed to pry it open halfway before Sabrina and Mason entered the room to investigate what was upsetting the dogs so much.

"Hayley, what are you doing here?" Sabrina demanded to know.

"I'm looking for Nykki," Hayley said.

"Well, she's not here," Sabrina said, eyeing her suspiciously. "Did you break into the house?"

"No. Of course not. The door was unlocked. Where were you?"

"Nigel asked us to take the dogs out for a walk while he went on a hike to clear his head after the service," Mason offered, a lascivious grin creeping onto his face as he folded his muscular tattooed arms.

"Well, where's Nykki?"

"I don't know," Sabrina said, "I haven't seen her since she ran out of the church when that awful

Vanda Spears started shouting her foolishness. Why? What's going on, Hayley? What aren't you telling us?"

Hayley took a deep breath.

How do you tell someone that her best best best best friend in the whole world was about to be booked for attempted murder?

Chapter 21

Dustin sat at the dining room table, tapping away at his computer when Hayley walked in with a bag of groceries and set them down on the kitchen counter. He looked up, stopped typing to acknowledge her with a slight wave, and then instantly went back to what he was doing.

"What's that you're working so diligently on? A History makeup test, I hope."

"I'm editing the footage I shot at your reunion. I must have uploaded three hours of stuff, but most of it's boring. Just a bunch of old people drinking and dancing. We'll be lucky if I end up with fifteen minutes that are kind of watchable."

Hayley had completely forgotten she had asked Dustin to record the reunion for posterity. At the last parent–teacher conference she had been warned that Dustin was barely passing a couple of his courses, so she strong-armed him into doing some extra credit for his Audio–Visual class to up his grade and do a little damage control for his overall lackluster GPA.

Hayley unpacked the groceries that needed to be stored in the refrigerator and left the rest of the unperishable items in the bag. She then joined her son at the dining room table.

"Dustin, would you play back all the footage you recorded that night so I can see it?" Hayley asked, staring at the computer screen, which was frozen on an image of Mona guzzling down a bottle of beer.

"All three hours? Are you kidding me?"

"I want to make sure there was nothing I missed that night."

"I already screened it for Uncle Sergio and he didn't see anything out of the ordinary watching it. Come on, Mom. I know you're mad I haven't cleaned my room in over a month but there are laws against torture."

"Fine. I won't make you watch it again. But I've got a great idea. Why don't you let me screen the footage for the next three hours and during that time you can go and clean your room?"

"I should have kept my big mouth shut," Dustin sighed, tapping a key on the computer and bringing up the raw footage he shot at the reunion. He pressed another button and Hayley watched as the first few reunion arrivals wandered into the main room of the golf club and made a beeline for the bar.

Dustin hauled himself to his feet, sighed again to make his displeasure crystal clear, and then stomped up the stairs, resigned to the fact that he was going to be stuck straightening his room for the time being.

Hayley sat there for almost an hour, glued to the computer screen, as more former classmates poured into the room and hugged and kissed and laughed. At the bar, she spotted Ivy's husband Nigel nursing a bourbon and making polite small talk with Sabrina and Nykki and Sabrina's boy toy Mason.

What was Nigel doing there so early?

Hayley distinctly remembered him arriving with Ivy and her cupcakes shortly before the murder.

Then it dawned on her.

Nigel had driven Nykki over to the reunion first since Ivy was still back at the summer rental kitchen putting the final touches on her cupcakes. Sabrina and Mason had gone to dinner first and were just going to meet them there.

Hayley remembered Nigel hanging around for a bit before he left to drive back to Seal Harbor and pick up Ivy, who texted him when her cupcakes were boxed and ready.

Nigel was so unassuming Hayley had completely forgotten about him being there earlier. She studied him closely in order to detect any unusual behavior or clue that he might have had murder on his mind, but Nigel seemed rather nonplussed and unengaged with the whole reunion until the DJ started spinning Gloria Estefan's 1995 dance classic, "Everlasting Love". Hayley watched as Nigel swayed from side to side to the beat and tapped his foot, looking around for some unsuspecting dance partner to pass by who he could grab by the arm and sweep out onto the dance floor. Most of the women were already on the arms of other men so his pickings were slim.

Hayley saw herself in the background, mercifully out of his reach, as she huddled with Mona by the bar.

Nigel couldn't help himself anymore. His arms shot up in the air and he began violently swiveling his hips as he slid out into the middle of the crowd dancing like some white disco suited John Travolta wannabe from circa 1977.

And he was gone.

Shaking his head from side to side.

Bumping into anyone who unwittingly invaded his personal space.

He was caught up in the moment.

Lost in the beat.

A few of Hayley's former classmates watched him in awe, impressed by his utter lack of self-consciousness.

Good for him for being completely and blissfully unaware of how silly he looked.

Sweat poured down his brow and he quickly wiped it away with the back of his hand. The song then segued into a thumping beat and Nigel was about to slink off the dance floor but he stopped midway when his foot tapped the floor, suddenly finding the rhythm of the next song as it rose in volume just as Gloria Estefan's iconic voice faded.

Nigel's eyes popped open as he identified the song.

Madonna's "Deeper and Deeper".

And he was back at it.

Gyrating and tossing his head back.

Screeching along with the Pop Princess.

Unbuttoning the top buttons of his shirt to let some air in so he didn't sweat so much.

Hayley let out an audible gasp.

Underneath his rather staid plaid dress shirt with the sleeves rolled up was a mat of chest hair.

Black.

Thick like a forest.

Hayley hadn't noticed it before because being the uptight English gentleman he was, his shirts were usually buttoned up to the neck.

The hair in Nykki's bed.

Could it be Nigel's?

It was possible that the mysterious phone call Nigel received at the funeral home when he was picking out a casket with Ivy's sister Irene was Nykki.

Further proof the two actually were having an affair.

Hayley paused the footage and grabbed her cell phone.

She immediately called Sergio.

"This is Chief Alvares," Sergio said on the other end.

His voice was scratchy and kept cutting out.

Hayley could barely hear him.

"Sergio? It's me, Hayley, can you hear me?"

Nothing.

Just more crackling.

"Hayley, I'm behind Dorr Mountain in the park. Near the South Ridge Loop. I have terrible phone reception out here," she could make out him saying.

"What are you doing all the way out there?"

More crackling.

"Hiker took a bad spill off a lookout point."

"Oh no. Was he hurt?"

". . . dead . . ."

"Sergio? Oh god, did you say the hiker died?"

"Hayley, can you hear me?"

His voice was finally clear for a few seconds.

"Yes, Sergio, I can hear you. Was it a tourist?"

"Your friend . . . killed . . ."

His voice cut out again.

"Sergio? What friend? Who are you talking about?"

He was talking but she couldn't make out anything he was saying.

Hayley was growing frustrated and more panicked with each passing second.

"Who, Sergio? Who? Can you hear me?"

And then the cell reception gods gave Sergio a few last seconds of clear reception before dropping the call entirely.

"Nykki Temple."

Island Food & Spirits
by
Hayley Powell

Yesterday while I was at work I received a reminder call about my upcoming coloring appointment with my hairstylist, Leopoldo ("Leo" for short). I was not about to miss this particular appointment because I certainly don't want to look as old as I feel at my daughter's upcoming high school graduation.

I never show up empty handed for my appointment because it's always best to keep the man in charge of your hair happy. So when I got home from work I checked the freezer in the garage for my little stockpile of mint chocolate chip ice cream cookies, which are Leo's favorite summer treat. He has been a big fan ever since I brought them to a Fourth of July barbecue a couple of years ago and he gobbled them all up in less than an hour. Now I make sure to have plenty on hand every time I see him because Leo bailed me out of a huge mess I made for myself a couple of years ago the day before a New Year's Eve party I was planning on attending.

I knew Leo left for his annual trip to his homeland in Italy a few days after Christmas every year like clockwork and I had forgotten to squeeze in an appointment before his departure date because of all the pre-holiday shopping and school activities. So I decided this year I would take matters into my own hands and color my own hair.

Worst. Mistake. Ever.

Two days before the party, I stopped by the local Rite Aid and, after much perusing and debating with myself, I settled on a pretty medium brunette with subtle golden highlights. One can never have enough highlights, especially during a cold dreary Maine winter.

That evening, after dinner and a few rum punch cocktails to relax, I kicked off the process of coloring my hair. After dousing my head and waiting the thirty minutes according to the directions on the box, I indulged in another one of my delicious Green Appletini cocktails to pass the time before washing that gray right out of my hair.

An hour later, I was blow drying my hair and then I collapsed onto my bed and promptly fell asleep.

When I awoke in the pre-dawn hours, I headed off to the bathroom, anxious to check out my fabulous new hair color.

That's when I let out a blood-curdling scream.

My kids nearly fell out of their beds and raced to see what horrible fate had befallen their mother. They stopped in the doorway, their mouths agape, their eyes as big as saucers, as I sat on the edge of the tub mumbling in despair.

"Your hair is green!" Gemma squealed.

"Actually it's a bright lime color with specks of brown. Like mint chocolate chip ice cream!"

Dear Lord, they were right.

My whole head looked exactly like the mint chocolate chip ice cream I use in my ice cream sandwich cookie recipe!

My first thought was to call in sick but that wasn't an option since my boss Sal was out of town that day for a conference. So I tucked my hair up underneath a baseball cap after getting dressed and drove to work, my mind racing, trying to come up with a way to fix this disaster. Leo wasn't due back until just before Valentine's Day!

I called the salon, and after much begging and a last minute late afternoon cancellation due to the snowstorm about to hit town, one of Leo's girls managed to fit me in and assured me she could dye my hair back to normal.

Finally a light at the end of the tunnel.

Albeit a bright green light.

Later that afternoon, as I slid into the salon chair amidst some gentle ribbing and chuckles from the staff, I closed my eyes and prayed my muddy brown color would soon return.

Suddenly my eyes popped open at the sound of a loud outburst of laughter followed by a thud as if someone had just fallen to the floor. There was Leo rolling on the hardwood floor of the salon in a fit of giggles after taking one look at my bright green chocolate chip mint hair!

Apparently, Leo's flight had been delayed a day due to the snowstorm brewing outside and he had just dropped by to check on things at the salon.

Totally embarrassed, I begged for his forgiveness and promised never to try anything like this ever again! He graciously accepted my apology on the condition that I swing by the following day with a plate of my ice cream sandwich cookies because the color of my hair was making him crave them!

I learned two important things that day.

1. Never, ever cheat on your hairdresser or you will be sorry.
2. If you're in a bind and *have* to color your own hair never have a Green Appletini or two before you open the bottle.

So my advice this week is to take some time for yourself and try my delicious Green Appletini while also enjoying some of my Mint Chocolate Chip Ice Cream Sandwiches. Just make sure there isn't a bottle of hair dye anywhere within reach!

Green Appletini

Ingredients:

1½ ounces Green Apple Vodka
1½ ounces Sour Apple Pucker
    Schnapps

In a drink mixer add ice, vodka and schnapps. Mix well and pour into a chilled martini glass and enjoy.

Mint Chocolate Chip Ice Cream Sandwiches

<u>Cookie Ingredients:</u>

½ cup room temperature butter
½ cup white sugar
½ cup brown sugar
1 large egg
1 teaspoon vanilla
¼ teaspoon salt
1¼ cups flour
6 tablespoons unsweetened cocoa
   powder
½ teaspoon baking powder
Pint of Mint Chocolate Chip ice
   cream

Preheat your oven to 350 degrees and place parchment paper on two baking sheets.

In large bowl add the butter and sugars and cream together until light and fluffy.

Add the egg, vanilla, and salt and mix well.

In a separate bowl whisk together the cocoa powder, baking soda then add this to the wet ingredients and mix well. The batter will be thick. Drop rounded tablespoons of batter on the prepared baking sheets and bake 10 to 13 minutes until cookies are puffed and dry on top.

Scoop out rounded balls of ice cream to fit cookies and put on pan and freeze until ready to use.

When cookies are cooled remove ice cream balls from freezer and with your hand flatten a bit to fit between two cookies. Enjoy right away or wrap them up to enjoy later.

Chapter 22

"Bruce, for the record I have zero interest in listening to you theorize about anything least of all about what you think happened to Nykki Temple," Hayley said while fanning her fingers through her recipe files in order to select an appropriate dish for tomorrow's column that she still had to put to bed before leaving the office.

"Come on, Hayley, hear me out. You know you want to," Bruce said, slurping his fourth cup of coffee in an hour while hovering behind Hayley and peering over her shoulder to get a good look at her computer screen.

Hayley spun around in her office chair and waved an admonishing finger in his face. "Stop trying to sneak a peek at what I'm working on! It's just a Food & Cocktails column. I am not secretly working on my own high school reunion murder story, okay, Bruce? You don't have to worry!"

"With your personal connection, it would make sense for you to try and write the definitive piece, and well, there's really no room for two true crime books on the subject, right?"

"Right, Bruce," Hayley said, barely acknowledging him with a sideways glance.

"I'm sure you're aware that the whole town is buzzing about who Nykki was hiking with on Dorr Mountain when she allegedly slipped on some loose rocks and fell to her death," Bruce said, pouring himself another cup of coffee from the machine in the corner while keeping one eye trained on Hayley for her reaction.

Hayley remained non-plussed, barely participating in the conversation. "I've heard rumors."

"It's more than just rumors. She was with Ivy Foster's husband Nigel."

"Yes, I may have heard that," Hayley said, plucking a three by five note card out of the red plastic box that served as her recipe file and placing it down on the desk.

She began typing ingredients into her computer.

"Nobody in their right mind believes her death was an accident," Bruce said, emptying the coffee pot and setting it back down in the maker.

"Well, luckily it's not up to anybody in their right mind to decide anything. It's up to Sergio and his officers to finish the police investigation so why don't we wait until they tell us what actually happened?"

"Don't be so coy. I know your mind is racing as fast as mine," Bruce said.

"Bruce, how many times have I told you to take

the coffee pot into the kitchen and wash it out when it's empty."

"I thought that was your job as office manager to clean up after everybody," Bruce said smugly.

Hayley glared at him so long and hard Bruce flinched, suddenly nervous. He crossed back over and snatched up the empty coffee pot.

"Fine. I'll do it," he said quietly as he headed back to the kitchenette off the bullpen in the back of the office. He stopped in the doorway. "Admit it, Hayley. You know as well as I do what happened. Nigel murdered his wife Ivy in order to be with Nykki, with whom he was having an affair, right?"

Hayley didn't answer him.

She just continued typing ingredients from her written card into her computer file.

"But then, Nykki, who maybe was aware of the plan to kill Ivy, or better yet, might have even participated in it, suddenly started to feel guilty. Yeah, that's right. Maybe she even wanted to go to the cops!"

Hayley couldn't help but listen to Bruce as much as she tried to make it look like she wasn't even remotely interested in hearing what he had to say. But she would be lying to herself if she didn't admit the same thoughts had already crossed her mind.

Still, she was not about to give Bruce Linney any satisfaction.

"So now Nigel was in a pickle. If Nykki talked to the cops, then he would be arrested and tried for the murder of his wife. But if something happened to Nykki before she had a chance to sing like a bird, then he would be in the clear. That's why he talked her into going on a pleasant hike up Dorr Mountain in the park. It was a beautiful day. The view from up there is spectacular. What a perfect opportunity. She never slipped on any loose rocks! He pushed her! To stop her from exposing what he had done to Ivy! It makes total sense!"

Hayley loathed to agree with Bruce.

It seemed plausible.

But she never blinked.

Never even looked his way.

She would bite off her own tongue before she told Bruce his theory sounded logical.

Why feed his monstrous ego?

It also did not explain Vanda Spears.

Where did she come in?

Did she somehow discover the affair and was blackmailing Nykki?

Was it possible that Vanda walked into the kitchen at the golf club and witnessed Nigel or Nykki or both bludgeon poor Ivy to death?

But Nykki was in the main room most of the night.

Nobody saw her go near the kitchen.

She was with Sabrina the whole time.

And what about Sabrina?

Why was she so spooked by Vanda Spears?

What made her so afraid of a crazy homeless woman?

As much as Bruce's story added it all up, there were still many missing pieces left.

Despite the fact that her own ego was dwarfed by the size of Bruce's, Hayley was still smart enough to know that she would be better and faster than Bruce at finding those key pieces that would finally finish the puzzle.

Chapter 23

"You know, I am never one to gossip especially when it comes to one of Sergio's cases," Randy said as he sipped his glass of Merlot at Hayley's kitchen table while his sister examined a head of wilted lettuce before tossing it into the garbage can underneath the kitchen sink.

Hayley went back to rummaging through the refrigerator, hoping to find enough ingredients for a side salad to serve with the sandwiches she had ordered from the Well Bread sub shop for the kids' dinner. Not the ideal choice for a healthy home-cooked meal for her growing teenagers, but both had made it clear they weren't hungry.

Besides, every bone in Hayley's body ached from running around all day. She was also still suffering from some nasty purple bruises on her back and thighs from her hard fall onto the pavement after pushing Vanda Spears out of harm's way from Nykki's attempt to run her down in Ivy's rental car.

Hayley waited for her brother to add the all important "but" to his last statement.

Randy savored the wine before swallowing it and then set his glass down on the table. "But . . ."

Music to Hayley's ears.

"I know you were close to Ivy and Nykki so I wouldn't feel right not sharing what I overheard at the police station when I took Sergio some left-over chicken pot pie for his dinner after he called to say he would be working late," Randy said, scanning the kitchen counter for the open bottle of wine before jumping up and refilling his glass.

Randy, of all people, knew Hayley was never that close to Ivy and Nykki, but she wasn't about to contradict him because she was dying of curiosity to hear his dishy news, and she knew her brother had to come up with a strong reason to share what he knew with Hayley so he wouldn't be overcome with guilt about it later.

"Sergio was in the interrogation room with Ivy Foster's husband Nigel questioning him about what happened to Nykki Temple on top of Dorr Mountain, and the door just happened to be open a crack, and well, I was walking right by with my pot pie because Sergio's office is just down the hall from there, I couldn't help but overhear them talking . . ."

Randy stopped momentarily.

Hayley knew her brother was wrestling with the dilemma of sharing confidential information with a civilian, but she knew in her gut he would sing like a canary because the two of them never kept any secrets from one another.

That's why they were so close.

If past history was any indication, Randy would start spilling the beans in five, four, three, two, one . . .

"Nigel admitted he had an affair with Nykki. They had met through Ivy a couple of times over the past few years, and there was a strong attraction, but Nigel claimed they never acted upon it. It was only after their arrival here in Bar Harbor for the reunion when they could no longer resist their intense desire for one another!"

Randy was also a fan of soap operas so he was overly fond of words like "intense desire."

And from the amount of black body hair Hayley had found in Nykki's bed at the summer rental house, she knew what was coming next.

"So they did it when Ivy was out buying cupcake ingredients. And kept doing it. Nigel's excuse was that Ivy was treating him so badly and they hadn't had sex in so long that he couldn't help but finally respond to the attention from another woman. But he was guilt-ridden over cheating, especially with one of his wife's closest friends, and Nykki was distraught too. She was haunted by a sense of betrayal."

"Well, that didn't stop them from having sex after Ivy was murdered," Hayley said pulling a large wooden bowl from the top of the refrigerator before chopping some cucumbers on her cutting board.

"How do you know that?" Randy asked, swishing his Merlot around in the glass before downing it.

"Let's just say I found a large amount of DNA evidence suggesting they had sex in Nykki's bed after the funeral because Nykki would never go more than two days without changing her sheets," Hayley said.

"Well, Nigel swears he didn't kill Ivy and he is convinced Nykki had nothing to do with it either."

"So what happened on Dorr Mountain?"

"Nigel told Sergio that Nykki invited him on the hike so she could break it off once and for all in person. She told him that given the circumstances it would be best if they no longer saw each other. The whole botched affair was a momentary lapse in judgment and that she was not interested in pursuing anything serious."

"And Nigel agreed?"

"Yes. They both wanted to forget the whole thing and get back to their normal lives. Then, and here is the weird part, she asked him to turn around and head down the mountain while she continued to the top because she was dealing with a problem and needed to think about how she was going to handle it."

"What kind of problem?"

"She didn't say. And Nigel never asked. He was just relieved the whole sordid fling was behind him and he could move on with his life."

"Do you think Sergio believed him?"

"I'm not sure. He tends to squint a lot when he's suspicious of a story, but I was out in the hallway and I didn't have a good view of his face. But if you ask me, I would bet he's lying."

"Why?"

"Because it's almost always the husband. And Ivy was a monster to him, at least according to all the reports from the reunion," Randy said, upending the bottle of wine over his glass to get every last drop.

Hayley, on the other hand, was a tad more willing to give Nigel the benefit of the doubt since he had come clean about his affair with Nykki.

There was a light tapping on the front door so Hayley stopped chopping her cucumber, wiped her hands on a dish cloth, and headed out the kitchen and down the hall to answer the door.

Oliver, the teenage son of the sub shop owner, stood in the doorway with a white paper bag stuffed with three long deli sandwiches. He was in a tattered Imagine Dragons t-shirt and faded jeans and was wearing a Red Sox cap pulled down so far it shadowed his eyes.

"Hi, Mrs. Powell," Oliver said, a thin smile on his face. "I put in a kosher pickle sliced in quarters for you, on the house."

"Thanks, Oliver," Hayley said, taking the bag. "I forgot to add a tip when I paid by credit card over the phone so hold on a second."

Hayley turned and called upstairs. "Gemma, could you bring down my purse? It's on my bed!"

Hayley had purposely not included a tip when she gave her credit card number to Oliver's father when she placed the order.

She also purposely left her purse on her bed upstairs knowing Gemma would be in her room when Oliver arrived.

It was all part of a calculated well thought out plan.

Randy wandered in from the kitchen with his glass of Merlot to watch the scene just as Gemma pounded down the stairs and tossed the purse to Hayley, who innocently began to fish through the bottom of it for change after handing Gemma the bag of sandwiches.

"Oh, hi, Oliver," Gemma said.

Oliver raised the cap higher on his forehead revealing a pair of gorgeous green eyes that sparkled at the sight of Gemma.

"Nice to see you, Gemma," he said, his voice cracking.

"Oh, you two know each other?" Hayley asked, trying to act surprised.

"We're in the same class," Gemma said, yanking one of the wrapped subs out of the bag. "Is this the turkey with pepper jack and no mayo?"

Oliver nodded, now at a loss for words.

Or remaining silent so as not to risk his voice cracking again.

"So you must be graduating, too," Hayley said, handing Oliver a few dollars and some spare quarters.

"Thank you," Oliver said. "Yes, ma'am. Finally."

"Must be a busy time for you. Finals. Cap and gown fitting. Prom."

There was a pregnant pause.

Gemma was still too busy ripping open her sandwich to make sure it was prepared to her specifications to notice what was happening.

"Oh, I'm not going to the prom," Oliver said casually, stuffing the tip in his jeans pocket.

"Why not? It's a once-in-a-lifetime event. I'm sure someone as handsome and charming as you must have girls lining up to go with you," Hayley said, eyeing Gemma who was still oblivious to the conversation.

Randy, suddenly aware of Hayley's master plan, finished his wine and folded his arms to see how this matchmaking scene would play out.

"Not really," Oliver said, embarrassed.

"Gemma, did you hear that? Oliver doesn't have a date for the prom. Isn't that a coincidence?"

Gemma suddenly stopped picking at her sandwich and looked up at her mother. "What?"

Hayley turned to Oliver. "Gemma doesn't have a date either."

"Mom . . ." Gemma said under her breath, realizing too late what her mother was up to and not having it.

"Oh. I thought you were going with—" Oliver said before Hayley cut him off.

"No. You must have received some bad intel," Hayley said. "She's totally free that night."

Oliver stood up straight and tried to deepen his voice to come off more mature and masculine. "Well, if you're not doing anything, would you want to come with me?"

"To the prom?" Gemma asked, incredulous, still not sure how this happened.

"Uh, yeah. I mean, no pressure. It's okay if you don't want to. I just thought if you don't have other plans, you might want to . . . you know . . . come with me?"

It was an excruciatingly long moment.

Had Hayley overplayed her hand?

Would Gemma turn him down flat and then there would be hell to pay for her brazen interference into her daughter's personal life?

Randy was holding his breath waiting for Gemma's answer.

Oliver was pale and swaying from side to side, ready to pass out from nerves.

Gemma just stood there in silence.

It was agonizing for everyone.

Especially Hayley.

And then, with a perky smile on her face, Gemma said, "I'd love to. Thanks, Oliver."

Everyone breathed a sigh of relief.

"Do you have your phone?" Gemma asked.

Oliver nodded and handed her his cell. She pressed some keys and handed it back to him. "That's my number. Text me tomorrow and we can work out all the details."

"Okay. That sounds great. Thanks, Mrs. Powell," Oliver said, beaming, before glancing at Gemma and catching himself. "I mean, for the generous tip."

He floated out the door.

Gemma shoved the sandwich back in the bag

and handed it to her mother. "I'm going to call Carrie and let her know I'm now going to the prom. As for you, Mother, I will deal with you later."

She bounded up the stairs.

Wasn't that something a mother was supposed to say to her daughter and not the other way around?

She wasn't going to worry about it.

Yet.

Hayley turned to Randy and smiled. "Now that's how matchmaking is done. And Oliver is straight. Not like *your* guy!"

"Yes, Sis. I bow to your impressive skills. You are by far the superior Dolly Levi!"

Chapter 24

Hayley stood at the edge of the rocky cliff as a strong breeze blew past her face. She surveyed the area, still impressed with the lush green foliage that stretched for miles. The icy blue ocean was within sight off the shores of Mount Desert Island.

It was still one of the most beautiful places she had ever been.

And it was her home.

She looked down at her dusty black hiking boots, which were planted a safe distance from the edge, but close enough for her to scan the area for something Sergio and his team of police officers might have missed.

This was the exact spot where Nykki Temple plunged to her death.

"We should have brought a six pack of beer with us," Mona complained from a few feet away. "Am I the only one feeling parched?"

"Have a bottle of water," Liddy said, plucking one from her fanny pack and hurling it at Mona, who managed to catch it in her hammy fist before using it to wipe away the sweat that was running down the side of her face.

Mona popped the plastic cap off the bottle and began chugging it down. Even though she only wore a light blue tank top and cargo shorts and some work boots with dirt smudged white athletic socks, it was still too hot for her, even with the cool breeze sweeping over the top of Dorr Mountain.

Liddy zipped up her fanny pack and joined Hayley at the ledge. Her hands were wet from the bottled water, so she dried them on her Sierra Club ready stylish hiking outfit with a khaki jumper and matching shorts that were accented with expensive boots and a snappy tan fedora to keep the sun out of her eyes. She looked like Bindi the Jungle Girl all grown up leading a tree house tour.

"It's so hard to imagine Nykki was standing right here just moments before she died," Liddy said solemnly.

"The ledge isn't sloped or anything," Hayley said. "It juts straight out. She would have had to have been really close to the edge in order to pitch forward and fall. And there's nothing around for her to trip on so I'm confused about what really happened."

"So you think Nigel gave her the old heave ho?" Mona said, swallowing the last of the water and crushing the plastic bottle in her hand.

"Maybe. But let's face it. Nigel's kind of a wimp. I have a hard time buying him dragging a woman as strong as Nykki over to the edge and slinging her over the side," Hayley said.

"What if she was taking pictures with a camera and wasn't watching where she was going and got too close like this . . . ?" Liddy said, marching right up to the edge of the cliff, pretending to snap photos with an imaginary camera.

"Be careful, Liddy don't get too close," Hayley said, her stomach flip flopping at the sight of Liddy hovering near the edge of the long dropoff.

"Or maybe she was taking pictures and didn't see Nigel sneak up behind her like this . . ." Mona said, charging up behind Liddy, arms outstretched. She stopped short of her, but the sudden move startled Liddy, who took a quick step closer to the edge. Her left boot stepped out too far and she stumbled, losing her balance.

Hayley was looking at Mona and didn't notice right away. "That would make sense if the police had found a camera lying around nearby or in the vicinity of the body, but they didn't."

Hayley suddenly, out of the corner of her eye, saw Liddy waving her arms in the air frantically, but before she could react, Liddy toppled over the side of the cliff, screaming at the top of her lungs.

Mona jumped and spun around, but Liddy was no longer there.

Hayley stood motionless for a few seconds, mouth agape, horrified at what she had just witnessed, but then snapped out of it and raced to the side of the cliff.

"Liddy!" Hayley yelled as she ran and peered over the edge.

Liddy was dangling from a thick tree branch that protruded from the rock face. It was bending and looked like it could fracture at any moment.

"Help!" Liddy wailed, her eyes nearly popping out of her head.

Mona hustled to the cliff's edge next to Hayley, dropped to her knees and then flat out onto her stomach, and reached down with an outstretched hand to grab Liddy.

Hayley, her whole body shaking with fright, called down to her. "Liddy, take Mona's hand!"

Liddy squeezed her eyes shut and shook her head, afraid if she let go of the branch with one hand she wouldn't have the strength to support herself.

"Come on, I can't reach you! You have to help me!" Mona hollered.

Liddy took a deep breath, gathered some courage, opened one eye to size up how far she needed to stretch in order to reach Mona, and then let go with one hand just as the branch cracked half way, dropping her out of reach another few inches.

Liddy screeched, closing her eye again.

She kicked her legs desperately trying to find some kind of footing beneath her but there was none.

"Liddy, stop struggling so much! The branch will completely break off!"

"I'm too young and pretty to die!" Liddy sobbed.

Mona inched a little more over the edge, trying to reach Liddy. Her whole upper torso was now hanging over the side. Hayley feared Mona would slide right off, taking Liddy with her so she dropped down and grabbed ahold of Mona's legs, allowing Mona to lower herself a few more inches where she was within reach of Liddy.

"I got her!" Mona cried. "Pull us up!"

Pull them up?

Who did she think she was, the Bionic Woman?

Hayley glanced back.

Next to her was a large pine tree.

Using her boots, she pushed herself against it while still clutching Mona's hiking boots. She pressed her back into it using it for support as she strained to pull Mona.

"Come on, Liddy! Hold on! Use the crevice as a foothold! You can do it!"

Hayley couldn't see what was happening.

She could only imagine Mona was now clasping both of Liddy's hands as Liddy struggled to find a space in the rock face to steady herself.

The muscles in Hayley's arms were burning.

She wasn't sure just how long she would be able to hang on.

The sun beat against her red face.

Straining.

Pulling.

Her eyes stinging from the drops of sweat that poured down from her forehead.

And then finally, she heard Liddy gasping.

Mona had managed to haul her up onto solid ground.

They were hugging.

Liddy and Mona hugging?

Now that was a first.

Liddy was safe.

Hayley was about to join in when something caught her eye.

Next to the tree that she had used as a back brace was a small bush made of leaves and twigs. Nestled in the middle of it was a piece of clothing.

The cops must have missed it because it was so far away from the scene of the crime.

If in fact Nykki's death wasn't just a tragic accident.

Hayley reached down and snagged it.

She held it up and studied it.

The small fabric was from a hiking shirt.

Likely a man's shirt.

The color was back country green plaid.

The edges were frayed.

Like it had been torn off.

Perhaps during a struggle.

"You saved my life, Mona," Liddy said, sniffling, still traumatized by her near death experience. "How can I ever thank you?"

"You can thank me by never mentioning it again."

"Why?"

"Because I don't want you following me around like a wide-eyed puppy and being all grateful. I prefer you being a shallow bitch that I can make fun of, okay?"

"Fine! Whatever you want," Liddy said, secretly happy she wasn't going to have to treat Mona differently now.

Liddy and Mona's hug had finally reached the awkward stage and they pulled away from each other, both relieved that they would finally be able to go back to pretending not to like each other.

Hayley pocketed the piece of fabric, her mind racing.

Was she wrong about Nigel?

Did Nykki fight for her life during her final few moments and tear the shirt he was wearing?

Was Nigel's wimpy husband act just that?

An act?

Was he instead a cold-hearted killer responsible for not one but two murders?

Island Food & Spirits
by
Hayley Powell

Recently, for the third time in less than two months I found myself rummaging around in my garage freezer searching for a bag of blueberries so I could make my very popular streusel-topped blueberry muffins.

I grabbed my last bag of frozen blueberries that I had picked the previous summer. Luckily, blueberry season was just around the corner so I would be able to stock up again since I was nearly out thanks to my cat, who also happens to be named Blueberry.

Let me explain.

It all started last spring when Blueberry went missing. It wasn't the first time. Blueberry had a habit of wandering off to his old stomping grounds on Hancock Street where he used to live before I adopted him. Usually, someone would spot him and I would drive over and try to wrestle him into his cat carrier, which was no easy feat since, let's face it, Blueberry is fat. Then I would give up and unceremoniously toss him in the back seat of my car where he would curl up and go to sleep during the short ride home.

So much for the cat carrier.

But on this day, Blueberry didn't go to Hancock Street.

I received a frantic phone call from Lenora Hopkins, who works at Bark Harbor on Main Street, a popular store for canine customers and their owners. Lenora was a bit irritated, breathlessly informing me that my cat was terrorizing her clientele. A few locals had come in that day with their dogs and let them roam around. Within minutes the dogs were yelping and whining and scrambling to get out while slipping and sliding all over the place. A quick investigation revealed Blueberry snuggled deep inside the dog toys stuffed animal bin. When the unsuspecting pooches poked their noses into the bin to find a toy, Blueberry would strike with his paw, claws out, scaring the poor dogs half to death!

With Lenora threatening to call animal control, I begged her to wait until I got there. Before dashing off, I filled a large Ziploc® bag with half a dozen of my streusel-topped blueberry muffins I had baked earlier that were sitting on the counter cooling as a nice peace offering.

That seemed to work. Lenora didn't call animal control. And she loved my muffins.

A few weeks later I got a call from the First National Bank. Blueberry was found sleeping on the bank president's desk. When he tried to shoo him so he could start a meeting with some investors, Blueberry, who doesn't appreciated being disturbed while napping, started growling and hissing and taking swipes at him. I raced over to the bank to retrieve Blueberry, delivering another bag of my streusel-topped blueberry muffins, which the president loved so all was forgiven.

Which leads me to my latest batch of muffins that I am baking right now to take over to the Episcopal minister with my sincerest apologies.

Yes. More Blueberry drama.

And this one was a doozy.

Apparently, Blueberry chose the minister's chair up on the pulpit for his nap. As the children's choir began to sing their hymn, unsuspecting Minister Joe went to sit in his chair and did not see the sleeping cat, who woke up hissing and spitting. He jumped at Minister Joe, claws out and attached himself to his robe. The poor man was so startled and scared he unzipped his robe to escape Blueberry's wrath and ran from the pulpit right down the church aisle past the congregation and out the door. Apparently, it was a sight to behold as I was told later by a friend who was at the service that Minister Joe was wearing only boxers underneath his robe.

I just hope there are enough blueberries in the state of Maine to make up for this cat's antics!

Today I am sharing my Streusel-Topped Blueberry Muffins recipe, and I know they're tasty, because at this point half the town has tried them and everyone has been very generous with their compliments.

Streusel-Topped Blueberry Muffins

<u>Ingredients:</u>

2 cups all purpose flour plus 2 tablespoons
2 teaspoons baking powder
½ teaspoon salt
½ cup room temperature butter
¾ cup sugar
2 eggs
2 teaspoon vanilla extract
½ cup milk
2 cups fresh blueberries

Pre-heat your oven to 375 degrees and grease a 12 cup muffin tin.

Combine the 2 cups flour, 2 teaspoons baking powder, and ½ teaspoon salt in a bowl and set aside.

In a small bowl sprinkle the two tablespoons flour over blueberries mix and set aside.

In a large bowl, beat together the ½ cup butter, ¾ cup sugar until light and fluffy. Beat in the two eggs and vanilla. Fold in your dry ingredients alternately with the ½ cup of milk just until combined.

Gently fold in the blueberries and divide the batter into the muffin tins.

Streusel Topping

¼ cup white sugar
½ teaspoon cinnamon
2 tablespoons diced butter

Combine sugar, cinnamon in a bowl, add the diced butter and mash together with fork until mixture resembles crumbles. Sprinkle on the tops of the muffins.

Bake in your preheated oven for 20 to 25 minutes or until a toothpick inserted in the muffins comes out clean. Let muffins sit for at least 5 minutes before digging in.

If you're lucky enough to have a few blueberries left over like I did, treat yourself to a wonderfully refreshing Blueberry Smash Cocktail. A friend gave me the recipe and, believe me, it will certainly chase the blues away.

Blueberry Smash Cocktail

Ingredients:

2 ounces vodka
1 ounce simple syrup
1 ounce fresh lemon juice
15 blueberries
1 mint leaf for garnish

Muddle the blueberries and simple syrup in a mixing glass (end of a wooden spoon works). Add the vodka and lemon juice. Fill mixer with ice. Stir and strain into a cocktail glass and garnish with the mint leaf. What a way to end any hectic day!

Chapter 25

Hayley pulled into the Shop 'n Save parking lot, which was packed with cars since it was right in the middle of the late afternoon rush. She didn't want to feed her kids sandwiches for dinner again, so she decided to swing in and pick up some chicken breast and fresh veggies to stir fry homemade fajitas.

She circled around the lot three times searching for a space to open up, but her parking karma was apparently off because five minutes passed and there was still nothing available.

Hayley was about to give up and call the Well Bread sub shop again, which she felt she was single-handedly keeping in business at this point, when out of the corner of her eye she spotted Edie Staples barreling out of the store, pushing a grocery cart filled with plastic bags.

Hayley turned the steering wheel of her Kia and slowly followed behind Edie like a coyote stalking a lost puppy.

Edie pushed her cart next to a squeaky clean white Ford Freestyle that was parked at an angle and taking up two spaces.

Hayley grimaced.

No wonder the lot was so full.

It was because of thoughtless customers like Edie Staples.

The Reverend's wife!

Hayley waited patiently as Edie opened up the back of her SUV and loaded her bags into the car.

She rummaged through one of the bags, taking her sweet time, before finally pulling out a box of Oreo cookies.

She glanced around to make sure no one was watching before tearing into it and popping one into her mouth.

And then another.

And another.

This was a fine time for a cookie binge.

Haley tapped the steering wheel with her left index finger, resisting the urge to lay on her horn in order to give Edie a start and get her moving faster.

Gemma and Dustin would be home soon, their stomachs growling, whining, and complaining about how starving they were.

It was almost a daily ritual.

Hayley scanned the parking lot to check and see if another space had mercifully become free, but so such luck.

Edie licked the chocolate off her fingers and shut

the back of her SUV, finally fishing her keys out of the pocket of her navy blue knee length skirt.

She climbed into the front seat, shut the door, and then began checking her makeup in the rear view mirror.

Hayley let out a silent scream.

She couldn't take it anymore.

She pressed the palm of her hand down on the center of her steering wheel.

The horn blared almost as loud as the fire department's noon whistle.

Hayley could see Edie jump in surprise before craning her neck around to investigate who was honking at her.

Hayley instantly plastered an insincere smile on her face and offered Edie a friendly wave while making sure her turn signal was blinking so Edie would put the pieces together that Hayley was patiently waiting for her parking spot.

Hayley sighed with relief as Edie put the SUV in reverse and slowly backed out of the two spaces she had been hogging.

Edie clearly wanted to exit the lot past Hayley's Kia so Hayley politely backed up to give her plenty of room to maneuver.

It still took three times for Edie, who was blind as a bat and had no business possessing a driver's license, to clear the spaces without bumping into the cars on either side of her.

Edie waved back at Hayley as she drove off, but Hayley wasn't entirely certain the Reverend's wife had any clue who she was waving at.

Hayley pushed her gear shift into drive to pull into one of the empty spaces when suddenly without warning, a beat up maroon Buick LaCrosse sped up from the opposite direction and squealed into Hayley's space, stopping directly in the middle and taking up two spaces just like Edie Staples.

Hayley gasped.

The driver must have seen her turn signal and just chose to ignore it.

What kind of rude person does that?

She didn't have to wait for long to get her answer.

The driver's side door of the Buick flew open and Vanda Spears hopped out, a proud, excited look on her face.

Hayley couldn't believe it.

Since when did Vanda Spears own a car?

Even a dented, scraped-up used one.

She rolled down her window and called out to Vanda, who was passing by on her way into the store. "Excuse me, Vanda, I was waiting for that space," Hayley said, keeping her cool.

"Snooze you lose. Just chalk it up to us being even after you nearly killed me the other day."

What part of saving her life did Vanda not get?

Hayley bit her tongue.

"Like my fancy new wheels?" Vanda boasted.

Fancy was perhaps a bit of an overstatement.

"Paid cash for it. Almost eight grand. They let me drive it right off the lot."

By the looks of it, the car was worth no more than three grand.

But again, Hayley bit her tongue.

"Nobody's going to be calling me a deadbeat no more. I have my very own car!"

Hayley was dying to ask the obvious question.

Who gave her eight thousand dollars?

Did she have a relative who died suddenly and left her some cash in the will?

But Vanda didn't stick around long enough to answer any of Hayley's questions.

She waddled into the Shop 'n Save, her head held high, brandishing a whole new lease on life.

And probably driving without insurance.

So if nobody died and Vanda did not win the Maine Lotto, then someone gave her cash to buy her wreck.

And Hayley had a very strong suspicion who that person might be.

Chapter 26

"I just want to take this opportunity to apologize for my boorish behavior," Mason said, scratching his flat bare belly while hiking up his cargo shorts with his free hand.

Boorish?

He knows the word boorish?

How unexpected.

Hayley stood in the doorway of the summer rental house, gripping the strap of her navy blue tote bag that hung over her shoulder, ready to swing it at his head at any moment if he tried to grope her again.

"That's all right, Mason. I'm here to see Sabrina. Can you go get her for me, please?"

"She's not here. She went to pick up some supplies at the store in town. She should be back any minute. Why don't you come in and wait for her?"

Mason stepped aside and waved his arm to usher her inside.

Hayley hesitated.

She didn't like the idea of being alone in the house with him.

The less time spent with him the better.

But she was determined to speak with Sabrina.

"Please. I promise to be a gentleman," Mason said with a sheepish grin.

Hayley sized him up.

He was lean and muscled, an agile acrobat, but she had long nails that could scratch his eyes out if it came to that so she decided to take a chance.

She walked past him into the house.

He closed the door behind her.

"Can I get you something to drink?"

"I'm fine. Thank you."

There was an awkward moment as they stood facing each other.

"Sometimes after a few cocktails, I can get a little out of control, and start acting out and being ridiculous, and that's what happened at the reunion and I feel really bad about it. I also had a few before Ivy's funeral," Mason said, eyes downcast, taking a real stab at sincerity.

Hayley nodded. "I understand."

"People say I take after my father, who was somewhat of a player from what I hear, but he died when I was a baby so I don't really know."

"Well, let's just forget it ever happened."

"I appreciate that. I really do care for Sabrina. I've never met a woman quite like her, and I would hate for my actions when I was a drunken mess to jeopardize that . . ."

"I won't say anything," Hayley promised.

"Thank you," Mason said, sighing with relief.

"I know we just met, but I'm already thinking of getting a tattoo of her name."

Hayley perused his heavily inked body. "You sure you have room?"

"Back left thigh," Mason said, turning around and raising his shorts to reveal a small patch of skin still untouched by art work.

"Well, that's very sweet," Hayley said, hoping this young kid just wasn't a rebound for Sabrina after her two failed marriages.

"Hayley, what are you doing here?"

Hayley spun around to see Sabrina standing just inside the door holding a recyclable bag full of groceries.

"Oh, good. You're home. I was hoping we could talk," Hayley said.

Sabrina glanced at Mason and then back at Hayley, not entirely comfortable with the two of them mingling at the house without her present.

Perhaps Sabrina knew more than she let on when it came to Mason's curious hands after downing a couple of cocktails.

Sabrina instinctively knew what Hayley was there to discuss.

She marched forward, blowing past her, and handed the bag of groceries to Mason, who grabbed the handle before planting a kiss on her cheek.

"Mason, could you give Hayley and me some privacy, please?"

"Sure, no problem. I'll put these away and go for a swim."

Mason eyeballed Hayley, not confident she was telling him the truth when she promised his unwanted advances would be kept between the two of them. He then quietly retreated to the kitchen.

"What is it you want to talk about, Hayley? I'm not in the mood for socializing. We just got through Ivy's funeral and now we have to plan Nykki's. I feel like I'm living some kind of nightmare that I can't wake up from."

"I'm here about Vanda Spears."

"Come on, Hayley. Enough about her. Why do you insist on taking her seriously? She's a crazy homeless woman who spouts rubbish."

"She's a crazy homeless woman who just bought a new car."

"So what?"

"Where did she get the money?"

"How the hell should I know?"

"I think you gave it to her."

"What?"

"You're paying her off to keep quiet."

"Now *you're* spouting rubbish."

"What does she know about you, Sabrina? Why has she been blackmailing you?"

"Hayley, I know I wasn't exactly a good friend to you in high school. Sometimes when I think back, I'm downright embarrassed about how I acted toward you. But I've tried to make it up to you. I've tried to be considerate and supportive and even help you out when you insist on sticking your nose into murder cases that should be handled by the police, but my good will only goes so far and I resent you trying to create some sort of scandal by linking me somehow to the horrible deaths of my two best friends."

"I never said you were in any way connected to what happened to Ivy and Nykki. The police are focused on Nigel, not you. But there is a missing piece here and I am betting it has something to do with Vanda Spears. You can tell me, Sabrina. What is it? What's the big secret?"

For a moment, Hayley thought she was finally getting through to Sabrina.

Her hands were shaking slightly.

Her lips quivered.

She opened her mouth to speak as if a confession was imminent.

But then the light in her eyes dimmed.

It was as if she was snapping into survival mode.

Choosing to go all in on the cover up.

Whatever that might be.

"I have nothing further to say to you," Sabrina said. "I'd like you to leave now."

Hayley debated holding her ground, refusing to leave until Sabrina talked.

But that would only aggravate the already tense situation.

Hayley turned around and walked out the door to her car.

She was going to have to find out what secret Sabrina was hiding some other way.

Chapter 27

When Hayley walked into the office of the *Island Times* after driving back to town from Seal Harbor, Bruce was there waiting for her, an excited look on his face.

"Chief Alvares just arrested the husband for Ivy Foster's murder," he said giddily.

"Nigel?"

"Yes. He found a golf club in his bag with specks of blood and it also had Nigel's fingerprints all over it."

Hayley stood there, shocked.

She knew Nigel was a suspect, but deep down she never really believed he had it in him to brutally murder his wife.

Bruce stared at her, a smug look on his face, overjoyed that for once he was able to show up Hayley with information on an investigation.

Especially given the fact he was the one at the paper officially being paid to write about crimes.

Hayley spun around and dashed out the door.

"Where are you going? We're out of coffee!" Bruce yelled.

Hayley didn't bother responding.

Why encourage the chauvinist pig?

Okay, it was her responsibility as office manager to keep the coffee pot brewing throughout the day for the reporters and photographers and especially her bear of a boss Sal, but it just rankled her that Bruce kept insisting on reminding her of it.

Hayley jumped in her car and drove straight over to the police station.

Sergio was out when she arrived at the reception desk that Officer Donnie, the tall, lanky perpetually in training young cop, was manning.

She asked to see Nigel in his jail cell.

"Sorry, Hayley, the Brit gets no visitors and that's final," Donnie said with a self-satisfied smile, already drunk with power after being left in charge for twenty minutes while Sergio went to get his hair cut.

Hayley anticipated this on the drive over and casually handed Donnie her phone.

He squinted as he read the text message on the screen.

It was from Sergio.

Tell Donnie I said it was okay for you to speak with the suspect.

Donnie cleared his throat and handed the phone back to Hayley. "Okay, fine, go on back."

Hayley brushed past Donnie, who stood up from the desk to open the door that led to the row of cells in the back of the station. "Thank you, Donnie."

She neglected to mention that she had Dustin text her that message and just changed the contact information so the number was identified as Sergio's.

She knew Sergio had a running appointment at the barbershop during the lunch hour the second Tuesday of every month to get his locks trimmed.

Hayley found Nigel sitting on a bench in the first cell.

He was crouched over, his head buried in his hands, and he was still wearing his golf attire, a bright green Polo shirt with tan pants and white golf shoes.

All that was missing was the matching Bucket Hat.

"Nigel?"

He looked up, his eyes red from crying.

He leapt to his feet and ran to her, gripping the gray bars of the cell. "Hayley, please, you have to do something to get me out of here! The chief is married to your brother, right? Can't you talk to him? I didn't do this! I didn't kill Ivy . . . or Nykki!"

"I believe you, Nigel, at least I think I do, but the golf club . . ."

"I know it looks bad . . ."

"The club was in your golf bag. There were specks of blood on it."

"I know! Someone must have stolen the club, killed Ivy with it and then planted it back in my bag! Please! You have to believe me!"

"It's a little far-fetched. If someone was trying to

frame you, how would they even know what your golf clubs looked like?"

"I've only played once since I arrived in Bar Harbor. I did nine holes with a nice gentleman I met at the club. I was there drinking to forget Ivy's constant nagging. I mean, scratch that. I don't want to incriminate myself any more than I already have!"

"I saw firsthand Ivy's treatment of you, Nigel. It's okay. That's not evidence you killed her."

"But it's a motive and I'm afraid that might be enough to convict me!"

"Okay, so this man you met at the club, what was his name?"

"Nice chap. McNally, I think. Yes, Charles McNally!"

Hayley gasped, floored.

Charles McNally.

The classmate who was still harboring a giant crush on Ivy at the reunion.

Still lovestruck after twenty years.

What if he approached Ivy before the reunion and confided that his feelings were unabated after all this time and she rebuffed him?

What if her rejection just caused him to snap?

Perhaps in his mind he thought if he couldn't have her, then no one would.

He must have found out Nigel was a golfer and just happened to run into him at the bar where the two became chums.

Once Charles made it clear he was an avid golfer, it would be natural for Nigel to suggest they play a round.

He saw Nigel's clubs, maybe pilfered one while Nigel wasn't looking once they were heading back to the club for a drink.

Then, at the reunion, after making a big show in front of Hayley about how he was still in love with Ivy and hadn't seen her yet, he snuck into the kitchen and bludgeoned her to death before slipping out, hiding the murder weapon, and then making sure everyone saw him go back into the kitchen to discover the body.

Later, he could have put the golf club back into Nigel's bag at the summer rental.

Yes.

This made complete sense.

And what if Nykki saw him leaving the summer rental after putting back the golf club?

That would leave a witness.

Maybe he had to take her out too.

Chapter 28

The tears streamed down Hayley's cheeks.

She swore to herself that she wouldn't cry.

In fact, Gemma made her promise.

But she just couldn't help herself as her daughter descended the stairs in her Princess Sweetheart floor-length tulle dress. It was gorgeous.

But it was Gemma who made the dress truly beautiful.

Her hair was styled in a classic up do with decorative bobby pins, her makeup flawless thanks to detailed instructions from her Aunt Liddy.

Her smile was radiant.

She was like one of those Disney princesses she worshipped as a child.

At the foot of the stairs, her date Oliver was dashing in a black peak lapel tuxedo jacket right out of *The Great Gatsby*.

If Hayley ever thought Oliver was slightly goofy, that myth was instantly dispelled by his miraculous transformation into a male model with his slicked back hair, confident posture, and handsome face, which glowed at the sight of his date taking his hand as she landed next to him.

Dustin, in far more casual attire, a *Family Guy* t-shirt and ratty shorts, circled the couple with his GoPro camera. His original plan was to follow the couple around all night and edit together a short film he could submit to film festivals, but his sister quickly nixed his lofty plans, not wanting her prom night judged by a committee.

Leroy, unimpressed, lifted his head long enough to inspect the dress, before going back to sleep in the corner of the couch where he was not ever supposed to be, but there was too much going on for anyone to notice.

Gemma grimaced at the sight of her mother's embarrassing waterworks, so Hayley fished a Kleenex® out of her pants pocket and blew her nose, honking so loud Dustin felt the need to swing the camera around and get the action on camera.

Hayley, wiping the tears away, motioned for him to stop recording her breakdown, but he didn't listen, keeping the GoPro trained on her to capture every dramatic sniffle. The budding director instinctively knew the heightened emotion was gold.

After Gemma patiently waited for Hayley to regain her composure, she gently asked in a soft, feminine voice, "How do I look?"

Hayley lost it all over again.

And a gleeful Dustin recorded every mortifying second.

"You know what, we should probably just go,"

Gemma said, giving her sobbing mother a quick hug before walking out the door which was held open by Oliver.

Dustin followed close behind nearly tripping over the welcome mat to make sure he got Gemma's reaction because he knew what was coming next.

Gemma stopped suddenly on the top step, her eyes wide with surprise at the sight of a silver stretch limousine waiting in front of the house. Standing next to the limo, in a gray chauffeur's uniform and black gloves, waiting to usher the young couple into the back of the limo that was stocked with snacks and non-alcoholic beverages was Aaron, beaming from ear to ear.

Aaron asked Hayley if he could treat the kids to a first-class ride to the prom as a graduation present for Gemma.

Hayley of course agreed, touched by the gesture.

This guy certainly was a keeper.

"Wow, this is so much cooler than going in my beat up Ford Focus!" Oliver said, squeezing Gemma's hand.

She smiled and gave Aaron a tight hug before joining Oliver in the back. Aaron shut the door and winked at Hayley before jumping behind the wheel and driving off with Dustin running out in the middle of the street to get the action shot of the limo disappearing down the street.

Hayley walked back inside for more Kleenex®, happy her daughter was going to the prom with a real gentleman and not that now notorious player, Nate Forte.

Before she had a chance to wipe the last tear from her face, her cell phone rang and she picked it up off the kitchen table where she left it to see who was calling.

"Sis, it's me," Randy said.

"You will not believe how beautiful Gemma looked, Randy. I was overcome. She's all grown up."

"I'll see for myself at the premiere party your son JJ Abrams is planning. Now you wanted me to call you if I ran into this Charles McNally guy you want to talk to, right?"

"Yes, did you see him?"

"I'm looking at him right now. He's sitting here at my bar."

"Keep him there! I'm on my way."

"Oh, honey, I don't think he's going anywhere. He just ordered his third bourbon on the rocks."

With the phone still clamped to her ear, Hayley grabbed her bag and raced out the back kitchen door to her car parked in the driveway.

When she arrived at Drinks Like a Fish, a quick five-minute drive from her house, she instantly spied Charles McNally planted on a stool, hunched over the bar. He was bleary-eyed and swayed a bit as he swallowed the last of his now fourth or fifth bourbon.

Hayley sidled up to him and slid on top of the stool next to him. "I certainly hope you're not driving, Charles."

He jerked his head in her direction and squinted at her trying to focus before frowning.

"Oh, hello, Hayley. Thank you for your concern, but I am perfectly fine. Life's many disappointments have trained me to be very good at holding my liquor."

"Well, I'd be happy to drive you back to your hotel if you want."

"Have you forgotten? I designed the Designated Driver app. Only problem is we have no drivers all the way out in this backward town. But I'm staying with my parents. I can call my Dad to come pick me up. So I don't need a babysitter."

"How long will you be in town?"

"I'll be getting out of Dodge just as soon as I can change my flight. I thought coming back for this reunion would be just what I needed to turn things around, make a fresh start, but it's just made things worse."

"Sounds like you're taking Ivy's rejection pretty hard," Hayley said, signaling to Randy who stood behind the bar to bring her a bottled water.

Charles stared at her. "What are you talking about? Ivy didn't reject me. I never even got the chance to talk to her. I went into the kitchen to tell her how I felt and found her dead on the floor. My whole life crashed after that. I can't believe she's gone."

Charles' eyes welled up with tears.

He stared into the bottom of his empty glass.

"So you never professed your love to her?" Hayley asked.

"No. Now I'll never know if she felt the same way."

Hayley studied him closely.

He could be lying.

He told Hayley at the reunion he hadn't seen his beloved Ivy yet and lit up when he saw the altercation between her and Nigel. He could have then gone into the kitchen and spilled his guts to Ivy. After she rejected him, he may have walked outside in despair. He could have seen Nigel's golf clubs in his rental car and stolen one while Nigel was distracted by the dogs. He had plenty of time to whack Ivy over the head several times, return the club to where he found it, and slip back inside the main room with his former classmates before going into the kitchen to discover the body.

This could all be a ruse to deflect suspicion off him.

But Hayley had known Charles McNally since they were kids.

In fourth grade when he wrote a dirty word on the chalkboard it only took Mrs. Olsen four minutes to squeeze a confession out of him.

He couldn't live with the guilt.

People don't change that much.

"Charles, the police found a bloody golf club in Nigel's bag. He's been arrested for Ivy's murder."

"I hope they fry him!"

Lucky for Nigel, Maine didn't have the death penalty.

"It's just that he swears he didn't do it and I'm inclined to believe him. And if that's the case, then that means someone used his golf club to kill Ivy and then planted it in his bag to frame him . . . and you did play golf with him right before the murder."

Charles slammed his glass down on the bar, startling a few nearby patrons as well as Randy who had just dropped off Hayley's water and was walking back to the kitchen.

He spun around ready to kick Charles out.

Hayley waved him off.

"How could you possibly think I would touch a hair on Ivy's pretty little head? I worshipped her! And I didn't know Nigel was even her husband until I saw them at the reunion together. He never mentioned his wife when we played golf."

"Well, I know how deeply you cared for Ivy and if she rejected you . . ."

"I just told you I never spoke to her about anything that was going on with me, the feelings that came rushing back when I heard she was coming to the reunion, how my heart sang when I learned her marriage was in trouble . . . I never even got a chance to see her before . . ."

Charles burst into tears, tapping his empty glass on the bar, desperate for another bourbon.

Randy chose to ignore him by pretending not to hear.

"I was so hoping we might be able to resolve the nasty business that happened on the last night I saw her all those years ago . . . when she broke my heart . . . perhaps start anew . . . but then I walked in and saw her lying there in a pool of blood . . . it was so awful . . ."

"Wait. What nasty business are you talking about?" Hayley asked.

"It was a long time ago, Hayley. I'd rather not relive it."

"Charles, it's only a matter of time before the police zero in on the fact that you had an opportunity to pilfer one of Nigel's golf clubs and you wind up on the official suspect list."

"But I didn't do it!"

"Then let me help you. Tell me everything. The more we know the easier it will be to put all the pieces together and clear you."

Charles raised an eyebrow. "Are you working with the police?"

"Let's just say I'm an unofficial consultant," Hayley lied.

Charles nodded, softening. He stared at his empty glass again. "I remember it as if it were yesterday . . ."

Hayley leaned in closer, and put a comforting hand on his arm, encouraging him to open up.

Charles sighed. "It was the summer after graduation. I was college-bound in the fall. Ivy had ended things right after prom. She said she didn't think a long-distance relationship would work since she was going to college in New York and I was going to be at Wesleyan in Connecticut. But I couldn't leave without trying one more time to convince her we could make it work. I showed up at her door with a bouquet of flowers and I told her how I was convinced our relationship was worth fighting for and she just laughed in my face.

She had no intention of staying with me once she got to college. She wanted to keep her options open. A light shut off inside me at that moment. It was such a turning point. I had been student council president. Big man on campus. And she just crushed my heart and obliterated my confidence. I became hopelessly insecure and that's what led to the cheating scandal at college. There was so much pressure to succeed and make the Dean's List and I just couldn't hack it. Ivy did such a number on me. Of course it wasn't her fault. I let her get to me. I should've been stronger. And to think after twenty years, I was ready to let all that go, try again with her . . . God, I'm pathetic."

Hayley squeezed his arm. "You are *not* pathetic, Charles."

"I sure was that night. After she dumped me, I gave her a ride to Sabrina's house. Can you believe that? After all the drama on her doorstep, I still acted like her lap dog. I just did what she told me. I was in a trance like it wasn't even happening. She was going to a party and didn't want her parents to know. So two minutes after she laughed in my face over the idea of us staying a couple, I was dutifully driving her across town like her own personal sad sack chauffeur."

"Did you go to the party with her?"

"Are you kidding me? The second we pulled up to Sabrina's house she was out the door without even a thank you. I was clearly not invited."

"I'm surprised Sabrina didn't invite you."

"Sabrina wasn't the one having the party. It was at Julian Reed's house."

Hayley's eyes widened. "Julian Reed, the actor?"

"Yeah. She mentioned in the car that earlier in the day they ran into him on Main Street and he was so handsome and charming and after chatting with him for a few minutes he invited them up to the mansion he was renting for the summer that night, which is why she couldn't tell her parents. They never would have let her go even if she went with Sabrina and Nykki. I never saw her so excited. She was going to party with one of her favorite movie stars."

Julian Reed.

The movie star who so famously drowned in his pool the summer after Hayley's high school graduation.

She was fuzzy on the exact date.

It was so long ago.

But she was certain it was around the same time.

And the fact that Sabrina, Ivy, and Nykki, two of whom were now dead at the hands of a vicious killer, met Julian Reed at his house around the same time he died was just too much of a coincidence.

Was all of this somehow connected?

Randy, feeling sorry for Charles, who was now just a puddle of tears, filled his glass with more bourbon, which Charles gratefully accepted.

"On the house," Randy said.

Charles smiled weakly and then downed it in one gulp.

Hayley gave Charles a gentle pat on the back and then jumped off the stool and ran out of the bar.

Chapter 29

"Hayley, we're very busy today, we're hosting a local mystery author's book reading and signing tonight, and I don't have time to indulge all of your whimsical questions," Agatha Farnsworth sniffed as Hayley stood at the reception desk of the Jesup Memorial Library.

Agatha Farnsworth was in her eighties and had been the chief librarian at Jesup since the mid-Sixties. Whenever she laid an eye on Hayley it was if the two were frozen in time, and Hayley was still the loud and chatty thirteen year old who was constantly shushed and scolded whenever she went to the library to check out a book.

"Agatha, I just asked if your newspaper archives have been converted from microfilm to digital files."

"Such big words, Ms. Fancy Pants. Why do you need to know?"

"Because I'd like to do a little research and I just wanted to make sure I'd find what I'm looking for on the library computer."

"You're going to be the death of me. Always coming in here and making life difficult."

Hayley bit her tongue.

She hadn't been in the library since an ill-fated bake sale that ended in a food fight.

It wasn't her fault, but she had still been too embarrassed to return.

But that was another story.

Agatha lowered her wire rim granny glasses to the bridge of her nose and sighed. "Fine. Yes. All the *Island Times* and *Bar Harbor Herald* files are on the computer and we have one available right now, but please, remember to keep your voice down."

"I'm here alone, Agatha. I don't even have anyone to talk to," Hayley said through gritted teeth.

"Well, in my experience, that has never stopped you before," Agatha scoffed.

Hayley thought of a few responses she could throw back at Agatha, especially since her kids weren't around and she wouldn't have to worry about setting a bad example. But she knew she couldn't be rude for fear of being ejected from the library by the Crypt Keeper. Plus she knew Sergio would never agree to allow her to read through the police reports pertaining to the Julian Reed case twenty years ago, so she had to rely on newspaper articles from that summer.

Hayley whispered as softly as possible. "Thank you, Agatha."

Agatha, eyes blazing, puckered her lips and with spittle forming at the sides of her mouth, let out a long, reprimanding "Shhhh!"

Hayley opened her mouth to apologize, thought better of it, and just headed for the stairs that led down to the basement room where the computers were stored. She knew Agatha was finally satisfied because she was able to scold Hayley at least once while she was in the library.

At least Hayley never felt old when she was around Agatha. She was still a young school girl. Albeit one with a big mouth and behavioral issues.

Hayley sat down in a hardback wood chair in front of a large clunky desktop computer from the nineties. The library's budget had been slashed so many times they had yet to invest in some newer sleeker models. Hayley tried a quick simple Google search first on Julian Reed's death but mostly just the conspiracy theories popped up.

It was his ex-wife who was caught cheating and got nothing in the divorce.

It was a disgruntled fellow actor who Julian got fired because he didn't want to be upstaged by the young stud.

It was the nut job girlfriend he dumped who bad mouthed him incessantly in the press and accused him of being physically abusive.

But there was no hard evidence connecting any of them to any kind of foul play.

Hayley then used a password Agatha had scribbled on a notecard for her to enter the library's archive and pulled up the actual articles printed in both local papers in 1995 documenting the case.

She scanned the paragraphs from the first report in the *Island Times*.

The police were called to the scene by the housekeeper who had discovered the body floating face down in the pool around three in the morning.

Blood contaminated the swimming pool from the victim's head wound.

Hayley jumped ahead to an article printed a few days later after the official autopsy report was released.

Drugs and alcohol were found in his system.

The police concluded that Julian Reed was impaired from the vodka and barbiturates enough that night that he probably tripped and hit his head on the side of the pool as he fell in.

The official cause of death was accidental drowning.

But since Julian Reed was such a big movie star an official conclusion wasn't nearly enough to stop the cottage industry of conspiracy theories that grew out of what really happened that night.

And perhaps all those fans and conspiracy enthusiasts were right.

Maybe the Bar Harbor Police Department got it wrong.

Was there more to the story?

So many years had passed.

Could fresh eyes find something the investigators missed at the time?

Hayley pored over all the articles printed about the investigation.

At the end of one written just a few days after Julian Reed's drowning, the last paragraph included a list of people questioned by the police at the time of the incident.

One name jumped out at Hayley.

A young handyman in his early twenties who had been on the estate earlier that day fixing a leaky faucet in the master bath.

Lex Bansfield.

Hayley's ex-boyfriend.

Chapter 30

"So how's the Puppy Whisperer?" Lex said, his voice dripping with attitude.

"His name is Aaron," Hayley said, clearing her throat, trying to pretend this wasn't as awkward as it felt.

Some months ago Hayley was forced to make a choice.

Lex or Aaron.

She chose Aaron.

Lex took it hard.

In fact, he didn't speak to her for months and she even caught him avoiding her when he spotted her milling about the bananas in the produce section of the Shop 'n Save by spinning around and hustling off in the opposite direction.

She couldn't blame him.

She broke his heart.

He had basically told her so to her face the night she dumped him.

Right after he saved her life.

She had felt painfully guilty.

They were good together.

But she felt something deeper with Aaron.

And she knew she had to keep following the path she was on to find out if Aaron was the one she was meant to spend the rest of her life with.

But she would be lying to herself if she didn't admit there were times she missed Lex and his rugged good looks.

His gravelly voice.

His sly, sometimes demented, sense of humor.

She met him when she ran over him with her car.

You really get to know a person when you rush him to the hospital.

Luckily his injuries were minor.

But his infatuation with her was anything but.

She resisted his advances at first, but he wore her down and soon they were dating.

Her kids adored him.

Her friends heartily approved of him.

Even her mother was a fan and she never took to any of the men in Hayley's life.

Especially her deadbeat ex-husband.

Her words. Not Hayley's.

It all fell apart when his boss died and he was left without a job. He left town. He returned to his home state of Vermont and it looked like he was out of her life for good.

But after only eight months he returned ready to pick up where they had left off.

The only problem was Hayley had already met Aaron.

Now she was standing in the front doorway to Lex's construction company shop located in a warehouse at the end of town asking for his help.

She feared he wasn't about to make it easy for her.

"Lex, I was hoping you might be able to shed a little light on something . . ."

"So tell me. Is he as good a kisser as I was?"

"What?"

"You heard me."

"I'm not going to answer that."

"You can tell me. I won't tattle."

"I didn't come here to talk about my boyfriend. Being here is uncomfortable enough . . ."

"You're uncomfortable? I'm not uncomfortable. We're friends, Hayley. We can talk to each other about anything."

Her fears were completely founded.

He was not going to make this easy.

He was downright enjoying this.

Like a cat taunting a trapped mouse.

"Lex, please, I just have a few questions for you . . ."

"Great. You answer my question and then I'll answer yours."

Lex rolled up the sleeves of his plaid work shirt, showing off his sinewy forearms as he folded them across his broad chest.

There was no getting out of this.

Hayley sighed. "He's a very good kisser."

"That's not what I asked. I asked if he's better than me."

"Why are you doing this?"

"Because I can," Lex said, chuckling.

"You've been waiting a long time for this moment, haven't you?"

"Oh, you have no idea."

"Fine. He's a better kisser than you."

Lex studied her face and then broke out into a wide smile. "You're lying. I can always tell."

"No, I'm not."

"Yes, you are," he said, beaming.

"I'm not!"

She was.

She hated to admit it.

Aaron outpaced Lex in so many areas.

But Lex Bansfield knew how to kiss a woman in a sensual way she had never experienced before in her life.

To the point where her knees buckled.

He used to have to hold her up so she wouldn't fall.

He knew he was the best.

She knew he was the best.

And he was going to enjoy forcing her to say it out loud.

"Yes or no. Pick one and we're done. Am I a better kisser than the Puppy Whisperer?"

Hayley hissed under her breath but loud enough for him to hear. "Yes."

"Thank you," Lex said, satisfied.

"That was cruel," Hayley said, shaking her head.

"Maybe. But it sure did feel good. Now what do you want to know?"

"Did you come here one summer in your early twenties and work on an estate?"

"Yeah. That was the summer I fell in love with the island. I had to go back to Vermont and work for my Dad in the fall but this place was special. I couldn't get it out of my mind. It took me years, but I finally got back here when the job at the Hollingsworth estate came up about six years ago."

"Do you remember who you worked for that summer?"

"Yeah. That big-time actor who died. Julian Reed. Guy was a big jerk but he paid well. Why do you ask?"

"I was reading some old articles about his death and saw your name."

"Yeah. I worked on the estate the day he died. I mowed the lawn and watered the garden and fixed a leaky faucet for him, but I was out of there by three or four. Took a few buddies and some six packs of beer in my truck to the park that night. I didn't even hear he was dead until the next day when I showed up to do some trimming and the place was swarming with cops and reporters."

"You mentioned he was a jerk. Did he mistreat you?"

"Not really. The only time he ever spoke to me was to give me orders or to complain about overgrown weeds or something like that. The guy was never happy. All that money and you could tell he was depressed and miserable. I never saw him smile once. Why are you so interested in him?"

"I'm not sure yet. I think there might be more to his death than what was in the papers."

"Well, if you're on the case, then that must mean you think he was murdered."

"No. I'm just trying to dig up all the facts. It could very well be just a tragic accident. Too much drugs and alcohol and a slippery tile next to the pool. Thanks, Lex."

Hayley turned to go.

"You should talk to Glenda Goodrich."

Hayley spun back around. "Who?"

"Glenda Goodrich. She was Julian Reed's maid at the estate he rented that summer."

"Was she there the night he died?"

"She was the one who discovered the body and called the police."

"Do you know where I can find her?"

"Listen, Hayley, she was already in her late sixties back then."

"She died?"

"No. She's alive."

"So she's still here!"

"I wouldn't quite say that."

Chapter 31

"Natasha, would you be a dear and tell Papa Frank we should be heading to church soon," the old woman said, combing her long thin gray hair with a wooden brush.

Hayley stood at the bedside and leaned in gently, "Mrs. Goodrich, my name is Hayley Powell and I'm here because—"

"Reverend Bishop always gives such a lovely sermon. I would hate to show up late. Now go on. Find Papa Frank. I'm sure he's outside sneaking a cigarette."

A nurse appeared in the doorway behind Hayley. She was rather rotund in a white uniform with a pink sweater over it and had curly blond hair and a sweet quiet smile. Her name was Ashley. Hayley had just met her when she showed up at the Bar Harbor Retirement Home on the outskirts of town and asked to speak with Glenda Goodrich. "Natasha is . . . was Mrs. Goodrich's granddaughter. She died of cancer ten years ago."

Hayley turned and nodded to the nurse.

She turned back to the old woman, who had set her hairbrush down and was now buttoning the heavy blue sweater she was wearing over her yellow nightgown.

"It's cold in here," Glenda snapped.

"We have the temperature up to eighty degrees, Mrs. Goodrich. You shouldn't be cold."

"Frank is always trying to cut costs by turning down the heat in the winter, but what good is having a few extra bucks in your pocket if you freeze to death?"

The nurse stepped closer to Hayley and whispered in her ear. "Frank was her husband. He died in '98 after a stroke."

"How long has she been like this?"

"When she came here, she was just a little forgetful. She'd mix up the nurses' names or be walking down the hall and stop, not remembering where she was going. But it's gotten progressively worse over the last five years. Alzheimer's is a terrible disease. Her body is still strong, but her mind is almost gone at this point."

Hayley knew it would be a fruitless exercise to question the poor old woman.

But she knew she had to try.

She spotted a tray of food on the credenza and crossed over and picked up a plastic cup of vanilla pudding. She scooped out a dollop with a plastic spoon and held it out to Glenda. "Would you like some pudding, Glenda?"

"Oh, thank you, Natasha. You're such a good

girl," Glenda said, closing her eyes and opening her mouth.

Hayley gently spoon fed her the pudding and then sat on the edge of the bed.

Glenda opened her eyes and gave her the once over.

"Natasha, you're not dressed properly for church. Go change into something presentable right now. I don't want Reverend Bishop thinking my granddaughter is some kind of two-bit floozy."

Hayley was in a conservative print blouse and khaki pants.

Hardly a floozy.

But she nodded and patted Glenda's arm. "I will. I promise. By the way, Mr. Reed called."

"Who?" Glenda chirped, a perplexed look on her face.

"Julian Reed? The man who hired you to clean his estate this summer? He wanted to know what time to expect you tomorrow."

"I don't know anyone by that name. Why are you talking nonsense, Natasha? Is this some kind of game?"

"You don't remember Mr. Reed?"

Hayley hated pressing her.

Even if the woman did have a moment of clarity, there was no indication whatever she said would be the least bit helpful.

The woman laid her head back on her pillow, her eyes floating up to the ceiling as she struggled to remember.

When Lex told Hayley that Glenda Goodrich

was suffering from Alzheimer's, she knew she had to come prepared. She went online at the office and printed out an old picture of Julian Reed in his prime from the Nineties. She hoped the sight of him might trigger something in Glenda's brain.

She pulled the picture out of her bag and held it up in front of Glenda.

"Do you remember him?"

Glenda lowered her gaze to stare at the picture.

She took her time.

Studying every part of him.

And then she smiled.

"Of course I remember him. He was so handsome."

Hayley sighed with relief.

They were actually getting somewhere.

"That's your Papa Frank. That picture was taken right about the time he joined the Navy in 1966."

"No, Glenda, that's the man I was talking about. Julian Reed."

"That's not Frank?" Glenda said, her eyes suddenly filling with tears. "Why don't I remember?"

The nurse intervened. "It's time for Glenda's nap, Hayley. I'm afraid you're going to have to leave now."

The nurse had every right to protect Glenda Goodrich.

Hayley's questions were clearly confusing and upsetting her.

And the last thing Hayley wanted was to make Glenda feel worse.

Hayley stood up and gave Glenda a gentle kiss on the forehead. "Thank you, Glenda. You get some rest now."

Hayley turned and started to follow the nurse out the door when Glenda said in a quiet whisper, "They have their whole lives in front of them."

Hayley whirled around. "What did you say, Glenda?"

"You know, those girls are about your age, Natasha."

"What girls?"

The nurse sighed and placed a hand on Hayley's arm to steer her out of the room. "It's really time we left Glenda alone."

"That bastard deserved what he got if you ask me," Glenda spit out, chunks of vanilla pudding flying across the room.

Hayley shook free of the nurse's grip and scurried back to the bed. "Who are you talking about, Glenda? Do you remember now? Is it Julian Reed?"

The nurse finally lost her patience.

She marched up to Hayley and grabbed her arm, this time more forcefully. "Let's go, Hayley, please."

Glenda locked eyes with Hayley, a grim look on her face, as the now angry nurse pulled her away toward the door.

"I would never say anything. Those girls did nothing wrong. And they're so young. Why would I destroy their lives?"

"Glenda, what girls? Who are you talking about?"

And then she saw the light go out in Glenda Goodrich's eyes.

"You tell Papa Frank to warm up the car before we go, Natasha. I'm not going to ride to church freezing my buns off."

The nurse finally managed to hustle Hayley out of the room.

After a quick apology for overstaying her welcome, Hayley raced out of the retirement home to her car in the parking lot.

Glenda Goodrich may have been mostly spewing nonsense.

But for a brief second, her thoughts crystallized into a very specific clear memory.

And it was enough for Hayley to finally start piecing together the puzzle.

Island Food & Spirits
by
Hayley Powell

The other evening my son Dustin informed me his class was having an end-of-school-year party and handed me a list of all the treats the other parents were making for their kids to bring. I instantly knew I would make my grandmother's Chocolate Angel Food Cake. An always reliable party-time favorite. One thing I knew for sure was I had plenty of eggs for it.

This past winter I had become a bonafide chicken farmer. It was never a life-long dream, mind you, but it has certainly cut down my grocery bill now that I supply my own eggs.

My elderly neighbor, Mrs. Adelaide Gray, who feared the government was systematically poisoning us through processed food, decided to grow her own garden, which eventually included chickens to lay the four boiled eggs that she ate every morning. She had recently fenced in her yard and bought five chickens from a local former. Other than my kids complaining about the occasional clucking and a few escaping through a hole in the fence into my own backyard that I had to toss back once I got over my fear of touching them, the whole enterprise was relatively harmless.

Slowly, I began feeding them stale bread or a few leftovers since it was snowy and cold and Mrs. Gray didn't seem to be paying much attention to them. I found out why a few weeks later when I ran into one of my neighbors at the Shop 'n Save and she informed me that old Mrs. Gray had up and moved to Florida about a month ago after a nasty bout with bronchitis during the first winter storm, and her house was to be sold. Her son would be driving up from Portsmouth and emptying it out soon along with the chickens, which would be removed by any means necessary.

Visions of chicken pot pies and chicken cacciatore and chicken quesadillas filled my head! I know I should have let it go right then and there, but I had grown rather fond of those chickens. I didn't want to see them

die! Besides, I always had this Laura
Ingalls fantasy ever since I watched
reruns of *Little House on the Prairie* as a
kid. And who wouldn't want fresh eggs
every morning?

I enlisted my friend Mona to help
me haul over the little coop from Mrs.
Gray's backyard into mine and the
chickens were finally safe and sound.
They actually settled in quite nicely. I
would let them out in the morning
and shut the door on the coop when I
came home at night. My son Dustin
didn't mind tossing out chicken feed
on the ground before school and filling their pail with extra food when it
was empty since there was still snow on
the ground and no bugs to be found.

Well, about a week later, I got home
from the office one night and fixed
myself a nice Friday night pitcher of
strawberry daiquiris to wash away the
stress from the work week. There was
a knock on the back door.

When I opened it I found myself
facing an angry group of neighbors,
almost too many to let into my small
kitchen, but I couldn't let them stand
out in the cold. Once inside, they
handed me a petition signed by everybody within three blocks requesting

that I do something about the chickens or have them removed immediately.

I was flabbergasted. The chickens were so well behaved and hardly clucked anymore because they were fed regularly unlike at their previous home. That's when they handed me an envelope stuffed with pictures they had taken over the past week. I was horrified!

One photo after another of my chickens on top of my neighbors' cars, sitting on their porch rails, pecking through their garbage cans and even one of them chasing a cat while they all left their "calling card" (yes, chicken droppings) everywhere they went and all over everything!

I immediately offered to make strawberry daiquiris for everyone and they happily accepted, but still gave me just one week to fix this mess!

Well, no one said farming was going to be easy, so I purchased some chicken wire and bribed my brother Randy and his husband Sergio with some of my Chocolate Angel Food Cake to come over and install the fence around the coop so the chickens could have a home and keep my neighbors happy.

All in all, it worked out well and it's nice to have eggs when I need them!

Strawberry Daiquiris

<u>Ingredients:</u>

Four 16 ounce bags of frozen straw-
    berries
2 cups rum (feel free to add more
    when you taste)
½ cup lime juice
1 cup simple syrup

Add the strawberries to a large
blender and then pour in the rest of
the ingredients. Blend until very
smooth. Pour into your favorite glasses
and be prepared to be wowed!

Chocolate Angel Food Cake

<u>Ingredients:</u>

1½ cups egg whites at room tempera-
    ture (10 eggs)
1½ cups confectionary sugar
1 cup cake flour
¼ cup cocoa
1½ teaspoons cream of tarter
½ teaspoon salt
1 cup sugar

Frosting

<u>Ingredients:</u>

1½ cups heavy whipping cream
½ cup sugar

¼ cup cocoa powder
½ teaspoon salt
1 teaspoon vanilla

First, make the cake. Place your egg whites in a large bowl. Sift together the flour, sugar, and cocoa powder three times (I know but this is what my grandmother always did), set aside.

Add the cream of tarter and salt to the egg whites and beat at medium speed until soft peaks form. Then gradually add the sugar beating on high until peaks are stiff and glossy. Add in the flour a bit at a time until fully incorporated.

Spoon cake mixture into an ungreased 10-inch tube pan and run a knife through it to make sure there are no air bubbles. Bake on lowest rack in a preheated 375 degree oven for 35 to 40 minutes until light golden brown and the top is dry.

Remove from oven and cool completely, then remove from pan and place on a plate.

To prepare your frosting, in a bowl combine all of the frosting ingredients and frost the cooled cake.

Sit back and get ready for the "Oohs" and "Ahhs"!

Chapter 32

"Why bring up something that happened so long ago?" Sabrina scoffed, nervously stopping to tie her shoe.

Hayley had invited her for a casual stroll along the shore path while her boy toy Mason was working out at the local gym keeping those impossibly ripped abs hard. Sabrina had hesitated at first, but ultimately decided to trust Hayley when she told her she wouldn't ask any more questions about Vanda Spears.

And she kept her promise.

She was now pumping her about the night Julian Reed died.

"I just remember that being a tough night for me. I thought you and Ivy and Nykki were my friends but then you ditched me to go to a party," Hayley said.

Sabrina took more time than necessary to finish the knot because she was obviously using the extra seconds to get her story straight in her head.

She finally stood up and gave Hayley a quick sideways glance. "I just don't understand why you're so hung up on that. We were young and shallow and frankly not that nice, but times have changed. *We* changed."

That was debatable, but Hayley wisely chose to keep her mouth shut.

"We matured. Don't you think it's finally time to let all that go, Hayley, especially given the fact that Ivy and Nykki are no longer with us?"

Sabrina zipped up her lime green hoodie over her black sports bra and launched into some light stretching while they were stopped on the path.

She was willing to do anything to avoid making eye contact with Hayley.

"I had no idea you were on your way to Julian Reed's house that night. I mean, he was my favorite actor. I had a poster on my bedroom wall of him as the air force cadet in *Flight School.* That was, like my favorite movie when I was in eighth grade!"

Sabrina froze in mid-stretch.

She hadn't expected to hear the name Julian Reed.

"I would've given anything to have had the opportunity to meet him. What was he like?" Hayley said casually.

Sabrina erected herself and continued walking at such a fast pace Hayley had to jog to keep up. She started to sweat underneath her own lumpy, misshapen gray sweatshirt she chose for comfort as opposed to trying to be fashionable like Sabrina's colorful number.

Sabrina, out of sorts, a panicked look on her face, was about to break into a full run to escape Hayley, but Hayley anticipated the move and locked on to her wrist.

"Sabrina, talk to me. I know you and Ivy and Nykki went to Julian Reed's house the night he died."

Hayley wasn't positive that's what happened.

It was more of a guess.

But by the look of horror on Sabrina's face, she knew she had just hit pay dirt.

"Who . . . who told you? Vanda?"

"Vanda? No, it was . . ."

Wait.

Vanda Spears.

It was all starting to make sense.

"Something happened up there, didn't it? Something ugly," Hayley said, releasing her grip on Sabrina, who was too shocked and upset to even move a muscle. "The three of you were there when something happened and he wound up dead in the swimming pool."

"No . . ." Sabrina protested half-heartedly, but mostly she was resigned to the fact that the secret was out.

"Were you somehow responsible for his death?"

Sabrina nodded slightly.

Just enough for Hayley to know she was right.

And then Sabrina let out a wailing sob and doubled over as if in pain.

But it wasn't pain.

It was more a sense of relief.

It felt so good not to have to keep all that dark

awful energy tucked deep inside her anymore. Especially now that she was the only one of the three girls there that night who was still alive and carrying around this long kept secret.

Sabrina fell into Hayley's arms and released twenty years of pent up fear.

It poured out of her being.

Hayley held her tight and rubbed her back.

Then Sabrina pulled away, wiping the tears away, fighting to regain composure. "It really wasn't our fault. It was an accident. But we were so scared . . ."

"What happened?"

"We ran into him on Main Street earlier that day and we screamed like groupies and begged for his autograph. He was so nice. He invited us up to his house that night. Can you imagine? Three local yokels partying with a major movie star like Julian Reed? We were beside ourselves! I mean, it was the most exciting thing that had ever happened to us! I really wanted to include you, but Ivy insisted just the three of us go."

Now in hindsight, Hayley was grateful for the snub because if she had gone that night, her life might have changed forever too.

"When we got there he was really sweet and polite and had pizza and beer waiting for us. It was like a dream. He even put on some Whitney Houston and we all danced and laughed and it was all so innocent. But before long, he disappeared inside the house and when he came out he was wearing just a robe and we could all tell he didn't have anything on underneath. He set down a silver tray and there were pills and cocaine and god only knows what else. He also had a bottle of whiskey and dared us to do shots. Nykki and I got a weird feeling and so we didn't take anything but Ivy was really into it and started downing shots and snorting coke and just going with it. Pretty soon she was a complete mess. We tried to get her to leave but before we could talk her into it Julian grabbed her and half carried half dragged her into the house to his bedroom. Nykki and I were so scared. We didn't know what to do. We sort of convinced ourselves she would be okay, but then we heard her screaming inside the house so we ran in and found Julian lying on top of her trying to get her clothes off. Nykki just lunged forward and gave Julian a shove and he toppled over and off the bed landing on his butt. It was almost funny. But it infuriated him and he started swearing at us and calling us teases and told us to get the hell off his property. So we got on either side of Ivy to help her walk and hurried out of the house. I thought that was the end of it. But then, just as we got to the pool, Julian came bursting out of the house. We were only a few feet from the back gate. We were as good as out of there. But he was wild with rage and told us we weren't going anywhere until we showed him a good time. He came at us, swinging his fists at Nykki, who managed to duck but he still clocked her on the side of the head. I didn't know what to do. I just started screaming. That's when Ivy just lost it. She threw herself at him and shoved him as hard as she could. He stumbled back, and somehow lost his footing, and then he fell and his head hit the cement pavement. I just remember this sickening crunch. It was so loud. I heard him moaning. He tried to get back up but he lost his balance and fell into the pool. We just stood there, watching him float face down, not sure what to do. We were afraid if we tried to pull him out he would kill us. So we ran out of there as fast as we could."

"Leaving him there to drown," Hayley said, putting a comforting arm around Sabrina's still shaking shoulders.

"We were up all night trying to figure out what we should do. Ivy wanted to go to the police but Nykki said, *no*. We'd be arrested and then we would never get to go to college or see each other again or live normal lives. We were just out of high school and had our whole lives ahead of us. We were so scared we would lose everything! We'd always be those girls who killed Julian Reed! So the next morning we made a pact never to speak of it again. We were the only three that really knew what happened there that night."

"But you weren't. I just spoke to the maid who worked for Julian Reed that summer. She was there and witnessed the whole thing. But she was so disgusted by what she saw go down, she kept mum."

"I had no idea . . ." Sabrina said, her voice trailing off.

"And then there was Vanda Spears."

"Yes. Vanda."

"She must have been hanging around the estate that night hoping to catch a glimpse of her favorite actor and she probably saw the three of you running away."

"The three of us never discussed it after that night. Not once in twenty years. But when we came back to town for the reunion Vanda started making trouble. She said she knew what had happened and wanted us to make it worth her while to keep her mouth shut."

"We all know about Vanda's personal demons she's had to deal with and at the time she probably never even thought about going to the police with what she knew. She was too wrapped up in her own crazy world, and my guess is she just lost track of you. Maybe she even forgot what she saw," Hayley said, sitting down on the grass of Albert Meadow just off the Shore Path next to Sabrina, who had planted herself and was hugging her knees tight.

"She's always been mentally unstable and practically lived on the streets so the odds of her having her own computer and finding us on Facebook were pretty much nil," Sabrina said.

"But when she saw the three of you back in Bar Harbor for the reunion, something must have clicked. The memory of that night somehow came rushing back to her and since she was always having money troubles and couldn't keep a roof over her head she saw an opportunity. That's why you paid her off with the money she used to buy her car."

"I wanted to go to the police from the moment she first approached the three of us and tell them everything, but Ivy insisted we give Vanda anything she wanted because she was afraid if the scandal came out her cupcake business would be adversely affected."

"And after Ivy was killed, Nykki remained convinced the best option was to keep Vanda happy."

"Yes. I told her Vanda would never go away. She would always come back and ask for more, but Nykki didn't care. She just wanted her to stay quiet."

Hayley couldn't imagine how difficult it must have been for the three women to be haunted for so many years, looking over their shoulders, frightened that someone might discover the truth and their lives would be over as they know it.

She felt sorry for Sabrina.

But at least she was still alive.

Ivy and Nykki hadn't been so lucky.

Which begged the question.

Who had it out for them?

And was it connected to the secret pact they made to never tell anyone the role they played in Julian Reed's death?

Chapter 33

If anyone was an expert on Eighties superstar Julian Reed, it was Randy.

When Hayley called him at the bar and invited him over for happy hour cocktails later that afternoon, Randy jumped at the chance. He swung by his house he shared with husband Sergio and picked up a box of old magazines and newspaper clippings of all his Hollywood crushes that he kept stored in the basement and rushed right over leaving his trusty bar manager Michelle in charge of Drinks Like A Fish.

Hayley had his favorite drink, a Mojito, waiting for him when he arrived and the two sat at the kitchen table sipping their drinks while Hayley pumped Randy for information that might shed some light on who might be the one targeting Ivy, Nykki, and Sabrina so many years after that fateful night at Julian Reed's summer rental estate.

"I was devastated when I heard the news," Randy said, licking the sugar off the side of the glass. "I remember I went into mourning for weeks. He was my favorite movie star of all time and he died right here in my home town! I couldn't fathom it!"

"I don't remember you being so upset over Julian Reed dying," Hayley shrugged.

"Of course you don't. You never paid any attention to me back then. It was all about chasing boys and partying with your friends. I could barely crawl out of bed I was so destroyed. That is until *Goldeneye* came out later that fall and I found a new obsession with Pierce Brosnan! You know how much I go for older men with hairy chests! I remember watching him in *Remington Steele* when I was a little kid but he didn't really excite me like he did when he first appeared on screen as James Bond looking so dashing in that tux and brandishing that Walther PPK and . . ."

"Yes, Randy. Pierce Brosnan. I remember. Can we get back to Julian Reed?"

"Sorry. I tend to get distracted when I drink Mojitos."

"When I was at the library researching his death I saw a lot of conspiracy theories."

"Oh, yes! They started coming out the day after he died," Randy said, standing up from the table and reaching into his box of mementos and hauling out a stack of magazines.

He set them down and began leafing through them. "Every week there was a new story. A crazy mistress. A closeted gay lover. His mother. His uncle. His cousin. His chiropractor. His massage therapist. I think everybody who ever came in contact with him was considered a suspect at one time."

"But the police concluded his death was an accident . . ."

"Yes. And they also said Marilyn Monroe died of an accidental drug overdose. That didn't stop everyone from speculating that the Kennedy brothers were there that night and killed her to cover up her affair with JFK."

"I see your point."

Leroy scampered into the kitchen and stopped to sniff at his empty bowl on the plastic mat with paw prints in the corner. It was the universal sign he was hungry and that he expected his dinner without further delay.

Hayley stood up and crossed to a cupboard in the far corner to fetch a treat since it was too early for his dinner. "Well, I think we know now what really happened that night."

"All these years those girls kept it to themselves. They never told anybody. I don't think I could have done that," Randy said, shaking his head.

"That's not exactly breaking news. You've always been terrible at keeping secrets."

"That's because there are only two kinds of secrets. Ones not worth keeping and ones too good to keep."

Hayley tossed a chewy treat to Leroy, who scooped it up in his mouth and sauntered out of the kitchen to find a comfortable place to gnaw on it. She then mixed herself another Jack and

Coke and joined Randy back at the table, who was flipping through an old magazine.

"Oh, I remember this story in the *Enquirer*! This one is from 1989."

"You always used to run to the grocery store with your allowance every Wednesday when it came out to buy a copy. Please tell me you don't read that rag anymore!"

"I will neither confirm nor deny," Randy said, slapping the magazine down in front of Hayley.

On the cover was a picture of Julian Reed, coming out of a modest suburban house, his hand covering his face as he avoided the paparazzi while a young blond girl, no more than sixteen, in dark sunglasses, her mouth agape, clutched his shirt sleeve. She had an obvious baby bump. Plastered across the front was the headline "Julian Reed's Secret Love Child!"

"This one was particularly juicy! It was all about how Julian Reed got an underaged fan pregnant and then paid off the girl's family to keep quiet because he was worried about his image!"

"Not to mention being arrested for having sex with a minor! Do you think there was any truth to the story?"

"Of course there was! Otherwise the *Enquirer* wouldn't write about it!" Randy said, a defensive tone in his voice.

Hayley gave him a withering stare.

"Come on, you know as well as I do where there's smoke, there's always fire! According to the *Enquirer*, the girl's parents were strict Catholics so an abortion was out of the question."

"So she must have had the baby!"

"Yes! And the gossip rags hounded her for months despite all parties denying she had any kind of sexual relationship with Julian Reed. She finally moved away to a small town in the Midwest just to escape the glare of the spotlight. Eventually, all the hoopla died down and Julian Reed went back to being a box office star until six years later, when he died. Well, that cranked up the rumor mill all over again and that's when one reporter tracked the girl down and got a photograph of her buying an ice cream for a six-year-old boy."

"Do you have that issue?"

"I think so. These are all in chronological order. If I didn't become a bar owner I could've been a librarian. And I'd be a whole lot cuter than Agatha Farnsworth."

Randy set one stack of magazines to the side and began rifling through the box for more before yanking out a copy of the *National Enquirer* from 1995. "Here it is!"

He handed the magazine to Hayley.

Sure enough. On the cover was the girl, now a few years older, more conservatively dressed and her hair in a bun, with an adorable wide eyed little boy who bore more than a passing resemblance to Julian Reed.

"Whatever came of this?" Hayley asked, studying the picture.

"Nothing. The girl denied the boy was Julian

Reed's son. There was no way to prove it. She certainly wasn't going to subject him to a DNA test. So eventually the story died on the vine. Another salacious celebrity scandal popped up and everybody sort of forgot about it."

Hayley studied the photo of the little boy.

What if the story was true?

What if this really was Julian Reed's son?

What had happened to him?

"Dustin! Can you come down here? And bring your iPad!" Hayley yelled before picking up Randy's now empty glass and making him another Mojito as a reward for a job well done.

After a few moments they heard feet pounding down the stairs and Dustin, sleepy-eyed and bored, ambled into the kitchen, his iPad in his hand. "What's up?"

"Weren't you telling me about an app you downloaded that can age a photo to see what a child would look like years later as an adult?"

"Yeah FutureFace. It's really cool."

"Could you show me what he would look like today?" Hayley asked, pointing her finger at the boy on the cover of the Enquirer from 1995.

"Sure," Dustin said, snapping a photo of the boy with his iPad camera and then opening the app. He set the device down on the table between Hayley and Randy and they watched in awe as the boy's face slowly transformed into a twenty-five-year-old man.

Randy grabbed the iPad and squinted at the adult face. "Isn't that . . . ?"

"Sabrina Merryweather's boyfriend! The high diver! You met him at the bar!"

Hayley then snatched up the 1989 copy of the *Enquirer* and frantically flipped through the pages until she got to the two page spread detailing all the salacious details. "Cassidy! The girl's name was Rhonda Cassidy! Mason's last name is Cassidy! It's him! He's Julian Reed's long lost son!"

"Since everyone denied Julian was the boy's father, he probably just took his mother's name!" Hayley said, throwing the magazine back down.

Dustin held out his hand. "What do I get for cracking the case?"

"A mother's eternal gratitude! Now get back upstairs and finish your extra credit for History so you don't have to go to summer school!"

Dustin rolled his eyes and shuffled out of the kitchen.

"If Mason found out Julian Reed was his father and somehow discovered that Sabrina, Nykki, and Ivy were responsible for his death he might want to exact revenge!" Randy said, downing his second Mojito excitedly.

"And that's motive and opportunity," Hayley said.

Chapter 34

"Sabrina, it's Hayley. Call me when you get this message. I need to speak with you. It's rather urgent," Hayley said, trying to remain calm.

She ended the call and looked at Randy.

"Do you think . . . ?"

"There's no reason to assume the worst. Sabrina may be preoccupied. She could be taking a swim and left her cell phone in the house or she's out running errands and didn't hear it ring in her tote bag."

"We should call Sergio," Randy said, grabbing his phone out of his back pants pocket.

"And tell him what? We *think* we know who the killer is? Dustin's app isn't one hundred percent reliable. It just tells us that the boy in the picture grew up and became a man who just happens to look like Sabrina's boyfriend. I've learned not to bring Sergio into anything until we have absolute concrete proof."

"Well, I've never learned that lesson. I'm going to

take the magazine and the photo from FutureFace and show Sergio. At least maybe it will get him to focus more on Mason rather than Nigel."

"Okay, keep me posted," Hayley said, grabbing her car keys off the kitchen counter.

"Wait. Aren't you coming with me?"

"No. I'm going over to Sabrina's summer rental to see if she's there."

"Hayley! Haven't you learned anything from all those horror and suspense thrillers we stayed up late watching when we were kids? Whenever the heroine goes anywhere alone, it never ends well!"

"I'll be fine. Mason has no idea we're on to him. As long as I keep my cool, he won't suspect a thing. But I can't wait for Sergio! There's no telling when Mason plans on striking again. Sabrina's life could be in danger!"

She was out the door in a flash.

Hayley almost broke speed records driving to the summer rental in Seal Harbor.

When she pulled up out front, all appeared quiet and serene.

She knocked on the door and waited.

No answer.

She tried the door.

It was unlocked.

Just like last time.

Sabrina certainly wasn't afraid someone might rob the place.

Hayley silently entered and walked to the big picture window that overlooked the property that ran down to the coastline.

There didn't seem to be anyone around.

She had heard Ivy's sister Irene had temporarily adopted her seven pooches while Nigel was incarcerated.

Hayley made a beeline to the bedroom on the opposite side from Nyyki's where she found the body hair in the bed that undoubtedly belonged to Nigel.

This room was well kept and spotless.

Sabrina had a mild case of OCD for as long as Hayley could remember.

The bed was perfectly made, the bedspread pulled tight so there were no wrinkles or creases.

A few beauty products were lined up in a single row on the dresser, all turned so their labels faced outward.

This definitely had to be where Sabrina was staying with Mason.

She opened a few drawers.

Two stacks of women's shorts and pullovers all neatly folded.

She crossed to the closet across the room and opened the door.

A few print blouses hanging on the rack.

No wire hangers.

Joan Crawford would have been proud.

There were some men's shirts hanging there too.

Mason didn't strike Hayley as a neat freak so she assumed Sabrina had ironed and pressed his shirts for him so they didn't drive her mad.

She was about to close the door when she noticed

something balled up in the corner of the closet. She reached down and picked it up.

It was a men's hiking shirt.

Back country green plaid.

It must have been recently worn because it was smelly and smudged with dirt.

And there was a tear on the sleeve.

Something had ripped the fabric.

It was the same fabric Hayley found caught on that tree branch when she was up on top of Dorr Mountain with Liddy and Mona.

This had to be the shirt Mason Cassidy wore when he killed Nykki.

He probably didn't even know it was incriminating, which would explain why he didn't get rid of it.

Mason.

Mason Cassidy was the killer.

He was the one who stole the nine iron from Nigel's golf bag.

He was staying at the same summer rental so of course he had access to it.

Hayley could hardly forget he was at the reunion because he tried pawing her and kissing her in the kitchen.

There was plenty of time for him to sneak back there when Ivy was arranging her cupcakes and whack her over the head a few times.

Then, when it was convenient, he simply returned the golf club to Nigel's bag thereby framing him if anyone found it.

That took care of Ivy.

Then he probably followed Nykki when she

hiked to the top of the mountain with Nigel, stalking her like prey, waiting until Nigel left her alone and made his way back down before sneaking up behind her.

Knowing Nykki, she put up a hell of a fight, which would explain his shirt getting torn during a struggle.

But Mason was an athlete, young and strong.

She didn't stand a chance.

He hurled her over the side to her death.

That took care of Nykki.

Now it was Sabrina's turn.

He saved her for last because in the end she would be the easiest to kill.

Especially given the fact she was sleeping right next to him.

She would never see it coming.

The torn piece of fabric from his shirt was the evidence needed to connect Mason to at least one of the murders.

It was time to call Sergio.

She grabbed her cell phone from her bag and called the station.

Office Donnie answered.

"Donnie, it's Hayley Powell. Get me Chief Alvares. I know who killed Ivy Foster and Nykki Temple."

"I think he's out. Hold on. Let me go check his office," Donnie sighed, annoyed.

He was probably eating his lunch and resented the disturbance.

Hayley waited.

"Give me the phone," a man's voice suddenly commanded.

She could feel his breath on the back of her neck and it made her shudder.

Hayley slowly turned around.

Mason Cassidy's eyes darkened as he held out his hand.

"I'm not going to tell you again," he hissed. "The phone. Now!"

Hayley carefully placed it in the palm of his hand.

And then he flung her phone across the room where it hit the wall and smashed to bits.

He stared at the dirty torn plaid shirt she held in her hand.

Chapter 35

Hayley sized Mason up and down.

If his face wasn't so menacing she would have thought he looked adorable in his sky blue shirt, navy chinos, and lightweight navy blazer with matching navy deck shoes.

He looked as if he just stepped out of a sail boat catalogue.

And then it hit her like a freight train.

She gasped.

Boating.

"Oh dear god, you've already done it!" Hayley wailed.

"What are you talking about?"

"You've been boating!"

"Yes. Sailing the high seas. I was probably a ship's captain in another life. I just can't seem to get enough of it."

"And you took Sabrina with you! Out past the harbor and to the dark choppy water away from where anyone on shore would spot you, especially the Coast Guard, and you shoved her overboard! Just like you shoved Nykki over that cliff! And then you simply drove off in the boat, leaving her to drown . . . just like your father did!"

Mason flinched at the mention of his father.

Hayley made a mad dash around him to escape but he anticipated it, blocked her move and grabbed her forcefully by the wrists to hold her in place. "It's a shame you couldn't leave it alone. I really liked you. I couldn't understand why someone so nice would be friends with those conniving, appalling bitches!"

"Mason? Are you here?"

Hayley and Mason momentarily froze.

Hayley's arms in the air.

Mason's hands wrapped around her wrists.

Their faces close like they were locked in some kind of dancer's embrace in the middle of a macabre waltz and the music had suddenly stopped.

Sabrina walked into the room.

The sight of them still like statues startled her.

"What's . . . what's going on here?"

Mason released his grip on Hayley but kept his eyes firmly fixed on her as he spoke quietly to Sabrina. "Hayley just dropped by for an unannounced visit . . . again."

"I saw that you called, Hayley. I'm sorry I didn't get a chance to get back to you. I was—"

Mason interrupted her. "Your instincts were right, Hayley. I thought about taking her out on the boat. It would have been so quick and easy. All

I had to do was ask her for a beer and when she was bent over the cooler I could just pick her up by the legs and toss her over the side . . ."

"Mason, what are you talking about?"

"But why rush it? I love it here in Bar Harbor. I'm having such a good time. Sightseeing in the park, gorging on lobster, whale watching. Tomorrow I'm even thinking of renting a kayak. Doesn't that sound like fun? If I knocked off Sabrina too early, there would be all this drama and I'd have to cut my vacation short. At least with Ivy and Nykki there was no real personal connection so the police didn't hound me too much."

Sabrina rushed him. "Ivy? Nykki? Mason, are you saying—?"

He slapped her hard across the face.

She yelped and fell back on the bed.

Hayley eyed the door.

But Mason was too fast for her.

He rushed over and slammed it shut.

And then he stood in front of it like a guard dog.

Trapping all of them inside the bedroom.

"How did you find out about how your father really died?"

"A little homeless woman told me," Mason sneered.

"Vanda Spears?"

"Once I figured out who my father was, I had to know the truth about his death. I never believed the official story. So I traveled to the town where it happened. Bar Harbor, Maine. And I started asking questions. I found the now retired real estate agent who rented the place to him and she happened to mention the crazy fan who constantly hung around outside the gate of the estate hoping to get a glimpse of her idol. That's what put me into Vanda Spears' orbit. She wasn't hard to find. I just had to drive up and down Cottage Street a few times before I spotted her pushing her grocery cart and muttering to herself. The good Samaritan I am I offered to buy her lunch. I managed to get her liquored up real good to the point where she started singing about what she saw that night. Three stuck up bitches running away from the scene leaving my father face down in a swimming pool to drown!"

"Mason, you don't know the whole story," Sabrina said, choking on tears.

"Shut up! You don't get to talk! It's my turn to talk!"

Sabrina buried her face in her hands and sobbed.

"Once you had their names, I'm sure it was easy to get close to one of them by following her posts on Facebook. Sabrina was a recent divorcee. Visiting her sister in San Diego. Maybe open to the idea of a fling with a younger man after a bitter and exhausting divorce," Hayley spat out.

"You came *looking* for me?" Sabrina screamed, infuriated.

Mason ignored her. He kept his eyes on Hayley. "She checked in on Facebook at an ocean front cafe and tagged her sister. I was there within ten minutes. I just happened to casually stroll by their table and stop to introduce myself. I made up being a high diver at Sea World because I knew it would be a real turn on for her. What woman wouldn't want to bed a stud in a rubber suit who swims with dolphins?" Mason said. "It was so damn easy. *She* was so damn easy."

Sabrina sat upright, eyes burning with contempt. But she noticed Mason's hands both rolled into threatening fists so she remained silent.

He had already hit her once.

"After that, it was a whirlwind romance. I followed her around like a puppy dog and heaped compliments on her about how beautiful she was, how lucky I was to have a woman like her in my life, blah, blah, blah. I didn't mean a word of it but it certainly did the trick. I had access to her whole life. Her house. Her car. Her old diary I found stuffed in the back of a dresser drawer. That was a real page turner. The desperate scribblings of an eighteen-year-old-girl with a big dark secret. Yearning to relieve herself of all that guilt but there was no one she could share it with because she had made this pact with her two girlfriends never to breathe another word about it. So she took to writing it all down as a way to deal with the trauma."

"So once the facts were confirmed, you set your plan in motion," Hayley said. "First Ivy, then Nykki, and now Sabrina."

"Yes, but unfortunately, I need to add one more name to the list," Mason said, abruptly turning his head to the left and cracking his neck. "You."

Before Hayley had time to react, Mason sprinted

forward, his hands outstretched, about to wrap them around Hayley's throat, but Sabrina was suddenly off the bed and seized a lamp off the nightstand and smashed it over Mason's head, shattering the lamp into pieces.

Mason dropped to the floor, blood running down his forehead.

"Sabrina, run!" Hayley shrieked as she jumped over Mason's body, grabbing Sabrina by the hand, throwing open the bedroom door, and dragging her out of the room, not looking back.

They were half way across the living room, the front door within reach, when Hayley sensed someone running up fast behind her.

Sabrina flung open the door and ran outside screaming.

Before Hayley could pass the threshold, she felt a tug on her shirt collar and then she was being jerked back inside.

She struggled in the iron tight grasp of Mason, who violently hurled her to the floor. Her head cracked on the hard wood and for a moment she was disoriented.

She turned over and looked up at Mason, who was now standing over her, his chest heaving, blood all over his face, a wild murderous look in his eyes.

Hayley tried to get up but he pinned her to the floor with a foot to the chest. Then he looked around, his eyes settling on the Paul Bunyan statue on the wooden desk. It was within arm's reach. He grabbed it in his fist and raised it over his head.

He gripped it with both hands.

He was going to bludgeon her to death.

Just like he did to Ivy Foster.

She fought with all her might to escape but he was too strong. He then dropped to one knee, using his other to pin Hayley firmly to the floor. He was close enough now to get the job done.

Just as he swung the statue down to strike his first blow, a loud gun shot rang out.

Hayley screamed and squeezed her eyes shut.

There were a few moments of silence.

When she opened her eyes, Mason was still kneeling there, the statue still in his hand, a surprised look on his face.

And then he toppled over, landing on the hard wood floor next to Hayley, breathing heavily and moaning in pain.

Hayley looked up to see Sergio, gripping his pistol, shell shocked that he actually had to use it.

Randy was in the doorway with a distraught, almost catatonic Sabrina, gripping her arm so she didn't faint and drop to the floor.

Sergio marched over to Mason and rolled him over. "Just a flesh wound. He'll live."

Randy left Sabrina quivering at the door and bolted over to his sister and leaned down and drew her into a tight hug.

"I thought I was a goner," Hayley said, fighting back tears.

"Did you honestly think I was going to let you

come here alone? Of course I called Sergio immediately and told him we had to get over here to
make sure nothing happened to my favorite sister."

"I'm your only sister," Hayley said, smiling.

"Semantics," Randy said, gently holding Hayley
close to him while kissing her on the top of the
head.

Chapter 36

Hayley drove Sabrina, who was too shaken up to do anything, least of all drive, to the police station personally. They had left a few minutes after Randy and Sergio, who drove off with Mason Cassidy handcuffed in the back of the squad car. It took that long for Hayley to try and calm down Sabrina, who wasn't having an easy time after such a close brush with death. But finally, her sobs and whimpering subsided and she was ready to go to the police station and come clean about everything.

Hayley felt sorry for the former county coroner, who just stared out the passenger side window the entire ride, a blank look on her face.

When Hayley pulled her car into an empty space in the police station lot, she turned to Sabrina, trying to find the right words to say.

"I'm so sorry you had to go through this," Hayley said in a whisper. "But at least it's finally over."

Sabrina plucked some tissue out of her bag and

dabbed at her cheeks. "I wish it was over, Hayley, but I'm afraid this ordeal is just beginning. We both know I'll probably go to prison for the part I played in Julian Reed's death."

Hayley was at a loss for words.

The idea of Sabrina Merryweather doing hard time was beyond comprehension.

With a steely resolve, Sabrina took a deep breath and got out of the car.

Hayley jumped out and rushed to catch up to her as she ascended the steps into the lobby of the station.

Hayley squeezed Sabrina's shoulder as a show of moral support.

Officer Donnie was there waiting for them and escorted Sabrina to the interrogation room.

Sergio came out of the booking room with Mason Cassidy, who had already been patched up at the hospital. He kept his head down, his face sullen, as Sergio led him to a jail cell, deposited him inside with little fanfare, and locked him up.

He walked back to Hayley.

"Booked him on two murders and two attempted murders. He's going down for quite some time," Sergio said.

"What about Sabrina?"

"I don't see the district attorney prosecuting her after hearing all the facts of the case. But I've been wrong before. Keep your fingers crossed."

Randy scooted out of Sergio's office where he had been waiting for his sister to arrive. "You look like you could use a drink. On me. Let's go to my bar."

"You're the best brother ever," Hayley sighed as she kissed him on the cheek.

Her cell phone buzzed and she scooped it out of her pants pocket.

"It's a text from Aaron. He's at my house waiting for me."

"Did you two have a date planned for tonight?" Randy asked.

"No. He probably just wants to fill me in on his night chauffeuring Gemma and Oliver to their senior prom. Raincheck?"

"Absolutely! Just promise me you'll tell me everything!" Randy said, smiling as Hayley turned and hurried out the door.

When she pulled into the driveway at her two story house on Glen Mary Road, she saw Aaron's car parked in front. She entered through the back into the kitchen but there was no sign of him.

It was quiet.

Too quiet.

The kids were obviously not home.

"Aaron?"

No answer.

She went to grab a bottled water out of the fridge when she noticed a note tacked to the refrigerator door with a Wonder Woman magnet.

Dustin loved Wonder Woman.

Come down to the basement was scrawled on a torn piece of yellow lined notebook paper.

Under normal circumstances, Hayley wouldn't have hesitated.

But she had just nearly been beaten to death by a crazed killer.

Her nerves were frayed.

She cautiously walked to the battered door that led down to the basement underneath the house. As she slowly opened it, the door creaking, the hinges in need of some oil, she heard music playing.

It was a ballad.

Bonnie Raitt's "I Can't Make You Love Me."

Hayley's favorite song from freshman year.

She played it so many nights on her CD player in her bedroom whenever one of her high school crushes ended in disaster.

The song still resonated.

She warily descended to the bottom of the staircase and gasped at what was around the corner.

Her basement was decorated in crepe paper.

There was a mirrored disco ball hung from the ceiling that slowly circled around a makeshift dance floor.

A card table with a blue paper tissue table cloth was set up with finger foods and a large bowl filled with a cherry flavored 7 Up punch. Next to it was a half empty bottle of vodka that was undoubtedly used to spike it.

Taped to the wall was a large printed sign that said, "Welcome Class of '95."

Finally, standing in the middle of the dance floor, his face dotted with the reflections from the disco ball, was Aaron, decked out in a retro powder blue tuxedo and spiffy black shoes.

He held his hand out for her to join him.

"What . . . what is all this?" Hayley said, stunned.

"Your senior prom was such a lousy experience for you, I thought it might be nice to recreate it and start all over. Only this time with a better date."

"Oh, you think so?"

"Come on! I bet that deadbeat you let take you didn't turn out to be a handsome successful veterinarian, now did he?"

"Actually, he's a very successful state senator now."

Aaron raised an eyebrow.

"Okay, that's a lie. I think he might be in jail last I heard."

"I just want you to have a happier night to remember. You deserve it."

Hayley just stared at him.

"Be honest. Is this coming off sweet or creepy?"

She laughed. "Maybe a little of both."

"Trust me. I was going for sweet," Aaron said, his arm still extended, his hand waiting for hers.

Hayley broke into a wide smile and then stepped over to join him.

He took her in his arms and she rested her head on his shoulder.

They held each other tight and did a slow waltz to the song.

"You could've picked a song that was a little more upbeat," Hayley said.

"Gemma told me this was one of your all time favorites."

"Yes. But whenever I listen to it I want to rip my heart out."

"Well, it was between this and "Do You Wanna Get Funky," by C+C Music Factory, and I figured with a slow song I'd get to grope you more."

"I love a man with a plan."

Aaron raised Hayley's head up with a finger underneath her chin and leaned in to gently brush his lips across hers once before going in for a hotter, harder, more forceful kiss.

Hayley's face flushed.

Her body shivered.

She felt warm and giddy.

And she hadn't even had one cup of the spiked cherry punch yet.

This guy Aaron knew exactly what he was doing.

And he was certainly right about one thing.

This was going to be a night to remember.

Island Food & Spirits
by
Hayley Powell

I am tickled pink to announce that I am now the proud mother of a bonafide high school graduate. And I'm just thankful everything went off without a hitch.

Well, almost.

Yesterday we all arrived early to the graduation ceremonies at the high school gym in order to get good seats to watch my daughter graduate.

In tow was my son Dustin, Gemma's Uncles Randy and Sergio, and honorary Aunts Mona and Liddy.

Mona was carrying a cooler, which she placed on the floor in front of her feet. I assumed it was for the congratulatory get together after the ceremony.

I was wrong.

I had stocked up on plenty of tissues since at times like these I tend to get a little emotional, and I had felt myself on the verge of tears all morning long.

As usual the gym was ungodly hot with all the family and friends of the graduates packed in to view this momentous occasion in their children's lives.

I couldn't help but think that it seemed like only yesterday when Mona, Liddy, and I were standing in the back hallway waiting to begin the march through the gym in front of our parents, family, and friends, wearing those green and gold robes and funny little hats with tassels.

I could feel the sweat forming on my skin in the stifling hot gym, so I was grateful for Mona's foresight when she opened her cooler and started pouring us all some ice cold pink lemonade into plastic cups from the containers she had stashed in the cooler to quench our thirst.

I grabbed mine and practically downed the whole glass in one gulp as did everyone else in our group (except my son who was thankfully nursing a soda)!

Suddenly my eyes bugged out of my head as the drink hit my stomach and exploded.

Oh my god!

She had spiked the lemonade!

All I could squeak out was one word . . . "Mona!"

And cool as a cucumber, she smiled and mouthed the words, "You're welcome!"

She then looked straight ahead at the stage with that smile still plastered on her face, casually pouring herself some more "lemonade" into her plastic cup.

I could already see tomorrow's headline in the *Island Times* . . . "Mother, Her Family, and Friends Arrested for Public Drinking during High School Graduation!"

I would never live that down!

I glanced at Liddy, who was sitting to Mona's right. She seemed quite content sipping away on her cool lemonade drink. I glanced to my left and saw Randy staring wide-eyed at me and silently mouthing, "I'm already feeling it!"

Sergio, seated to Randy's left, wouldn't even look at me. He was the chief of police and he didn't want to arrest himself so he gently set his cup of "lemonade" down by his feet and pretended to ignore the rest of us.

I just shook my head and thought to myself, "Well, when in Rome . . ."

I held out my glass so Mona could top it off one more time as the band played the Marching Song and the graduates filed into the gym.

I'm happy to report that I wasn't a complete mess either as my daughter walked across the stage to accept her diploma. But everyone else was. I passed out tissues left and right to Randy, Sergio, Mona, and Liddy, who were all bawling. We applauded and cheered as Gemma accepted her diploma and turned to give us a bright smile and a big thumbs up.

After the ceremony, we all headed to the cafeteria, where everyone was invited to have snacks that the parents brought and to take lots of pictures of the proud and happy graduates.

I had been feeling a little nostalgic lately with everything that had been going on, so I decided to make Ivy's famous vanilla cupcakes with bright pink frosting, which had always been her favorite color, to bring to the festivities. They just seemed to scream party, and I know she would have loved it.

As my daughter and her best friend Carrie ran up to us, I finally got the opportunity to get a few pictures of the girls together.

As I lifted the camera up to snap a few photos, I suddenly felt the years melting away as I looked at the two smiling girls in front of me with their arms around each other, laughing into the camera, their futures still so bright, their whole lives ahead of them. For a split second I could see Ivy and Nykki smiling into a camera twenty years ago, feeling the exact same way and it made me smile.

It was a bittersweet moment, of course, but justice had been served. I said a quick prayer to myself for my old classmates, and returned my thoughts to the present because it was now time to enjoy this special day for the Class of 2015! I love you, Gemma! Mama's so proud!

She will hate that I included that last part.

Pink Lemonade Cocktail

<u>Ingredients:</u>

2 ounces pink lemonade
2 ounces cranberry juice
Splash of Triple Sec

Pour ingredients in an ice filled mixer glass, shake until chilled. Strain into a chilled glass and enjoy with friends.

Ivy's Famous Pink Frosted Cupcakes

<u>Ingredients:</u>

2¼ cups flour
1¾ cups sugar
1 tablespoon baking powder
½ teaspoon kosher salt
1 stick room temperature butter
¾ cup milk
2 large eggs
2 teaspoons vanilla extract

Add all your dry ingredients to a mixing bowl and mix together.

Then add the butter, milk, eggs, and vanilla to the dry ingredients and blend until all mixed together.

Line two muffin tins with cupcake liners and divide the batter into 18 cupcakes.

Bake in a preheated 350 degree oven for 20 minutes or until cupcakes spring back when touched on top.

Remove from oven and cool completely.

Pink Butter Cream Frosting

Ingredients:

3 sticks room temperature butter
2 cups confectionary sugar
2 teaspoons vanilla
pink food coloring

Add all ingredients to a bowl and beat until creamy. Add a few drops of pink food coloring and mix together. You can add more or less food coloring to get your desired pink color. Frost the cooled cupcakes and share with your friends!

Index of Recipes

Dreamsicle Cocktail   35

Dreamy Orange Dreamsicle Cake   35

Cape Codder   94

Cranberry Cream Cheese Bars   95

Summer Lemonade Cocktail   144

Lemon Tart   145

Green Appletini   183

Mint Chocolate Chip Ice Cream   184
 Sandwich Cookies

Streusel-Topped Blueberry Muffins   214

Blueberry Smash Cocktail   215

Strawberry Daiquiris   267

Chocolate Angel Food Cake   267

Pink Lemonade Cocktail   309

Ivy's Famous Pink Frosted Cupcakes   310

Dear Reader:

We hope you've enjoyed Hayley Powell's latest mystery, *Death of a Cupcake Queen*. And be sure to try out all those sweet and tasty dessert recipes Hayley wrote about in her columns.

Up next, Hayley shifts gears from sweets to mouth watering bacon recipes in her sizzling new adventure *Death of a Bacon Heiress*, coming soon from Kensington.

When we return to the picturesque coastal town of Bar Harbor, Maine, food columnist and amateur sleuth Hayley Powell is thrilled over receiving a call from a New York-based television producer who wants to fly her to New York to do a cooking demonstration on a nationally broadcast talk show.

While in the Big Apple, Hayley runs into Olivia Redmond, a billionaire heiress to Redmond Meats, known around the world for their top selling bacon products. Olivia summers in Bar Harbor with her handsome polo playing Argentinean husband at the seaside estate her family has owned for decades. Olivia is a rather eccentric character and is famous with the locals for walking her pet, a pot-bellied pig named Pork Chop, around town on a leash. She and Hayley become fast friends bonding over Hayley's Bacon Wrapped Jalapeno Stuffed Chicken Thighs that she prepared for her TV show segment and Olivia offers her a part time job on the spot blogging her bacon recipes for the Redmond Meats website.

But before Hayley can post her first recipe, Bacon Stripped Pancakes, Olivia turns up dead in the gardens of her summer estate, her grieving pet pig by her side. And she didn't die from eating too much greasy bacon. Someone snapped her neck, killing her instantly! Hayley immediately starts looking into Olivia's wealthy background. Did her ne'er-do-well Latin husband tire of catering to her every whim? Was it her bitter actor wannabe son who she cut off when he didn't go into the family business? Or maybe his scheming gold-digging girlfriend who is a Downton Abbey fan and desperate to become the lady of the manor? Could it have been someone on the company's board of directors who wanted to get rid of her tie-breaking vote? With the list of suspects growing, Hayley Powell is on the case.

Be sure to visit our website www.LeeHollis Mysteries.com and follow us on our Facebook page by typing in Lee Hollis.

Your Author in Crime,
Lee Hollis

GREAT BOOKS,
GREAT SAVINGS!

When You Visit Our Website:
www.kensingtonbooks.com
You Can Save Money Off The Retail Price
Of Any Book You Purchase!

- All Your Favorite Kensington Authors
- New Releases & Timeless Classics
- Overnight Shipping Available
- eBooks Available For Many Titles
- All Major Credit Cards Accepted

Visit Us Today To Start Saving!
www.kensingtonbooks.com

All Orders Are Subject To Availability.
Shipping and Handling Charges Apply.
Offers and Prices Subject To Change Without Notice.